JAY STRINGER

RUNAWAY TOWN

THOMAS & MERCER

Extract from *Nineteen Eighty-Four* by George Orwell (Copyright © George Orwell, 1949) by permission of Bill Hamilton as the Literary Executor of the Estate of the Late Sonia Brownell Orwell.

Published by Thomas & Mercer
PO Box 400818
Las Vegas, NV 89140

ISBN-13: 9781612183398
ISBN-10: 1612183395
Library of Congress Control Number: 2012917234

Under the spreading chestnut tree, I sold you and you sold me.

—GEORGE ORWELL

Flames rise around the corners.

Dancing red and yellow. They roar like a lion. It hurts my ears.

I'm four years old. This is the first time I've seen my family burned out of our home.

I cling onto my mother's arm with both hands. I'm scared, but I can't take my eyes away from the flames.

From inside the caravan comes blackness. A living cloud that follows the flames out and chokes the air around it.

It spreads toward us. I bury my face in my mother's side, but my father pulls me to stand with my brother. He points us toward the flames.

"Remember this," he says. "Na bister."

Other families gather round. Some of their homes are also burning. Those who haven't been burned out are packing up. Getting ready to move on. Again.

My mother wraps me in a blanket and sings to me. The other women who travel with us sing traditional songs, songs of our people. My mother's songs are different, and in a few years I'll understand why.

But right now I'm only four years old.

My home is burning.

It starts here.

ONE

The man driving the car wasn't much for conversation. That was fine with me. To paraphrase a song lyric, I like awkward silences because I grew up in denial. I eased back into my seat and watched the scenery fly by.

He'd barely waited for me to sit down before he pulled away from the curb. He didn't say where we were going, but he didn't need to; when you've sold your soul, you're just along for the ride… And I had a feeling where this ride would end. I was in deep with the Gaines family.

As far as crime in the Black Country went, the Gaines family was old money, connected through Ireland and eastern Scotland, with enough muscle to keep the Birmingham gangs at bay. The head of the family was Ransford Gaines. I didn't know him well, but he and my father went back to the seventies. I'd never asked too many questions about the family connection, for the same simple reason I was keeping quiet now. The song lyric said it all. The Hold Steady had written the story of my life with that one.

These days, his eldest was running things. Veronica Gaines: tall, good looking, trouble. My mother had always warned me about women like Veronica, but when was the last time anyone listened to their mother?

The thought of seeing Gaines made my stomach hurt, and I rooted in my pockets for my prescription, trying to keep the pain off my face. No need for the driver to know that a madman had rearranged my insides with a knife five months earlier, or that the doctors had spliced me together like a faulty electrical cable. No need for him to know that the same attack had left me with a nice scar down my leg and a knee that hated me. I felt my hand shake slightly as it held the pill bottle and wondered which ones I'd remembered to bring. I was hooked on:

Pills for my digestion.

Pills for the pain.

Pills to sleep.

The booze and the coffee had been replaced with:

Orange juice.

Peppermint tea.

Ginger biscuits.

I could medicate my stomach and ignore my knee, but nothing eased my nightmares. Some nights I dreamed of the attack and the pain. Some nights I dreamed of the blood. Every night I returned to the same dream, the flames. Flames that were as old as I was, flames that had followed my family each time we moved.

Every night the dreams would drive me out into the darkness for a walk. And I guess the walks had become so regular that people had been able to predict them. As I'd rounded the corner near my flat, the black car had slid up to the curb next to me.

"Get in," said the driver. "The boss wants a word."

What the hell.

I had something better to do?

TWO

My chauffeur-driven car pulled up outside of Legs, the Wolverhampton nightclub owned by the Gaines family. It was off the books, hidden above and behind a row of shops on Broad Street. There were no licenses to apply for, no tax forms to fill out, and no laws to follow. Both the council and the police knew it was there, but it was the perfect solution for both of them. If they turned a blind eye, then the illegal stuff was kept off the streets, and crime statistics stayed down. Back when I'd been a cop, I'd learned the hard way that stats rule the world.

It was all part of the game.

Bull was waiting by the door as we pulled up at the back of the club. Five times bigger than Jesus and twice as scary, he was Veronica Gaines's right-hand man. He'd been a small-time pro wrestler on the British circuit when he killed somebody in the ring in Blackpool.

He clamped his bearlike grip on my shoulder and pushed me ahead of him, through the open door and into the heart of the club. Like much of the Gaines operation, Legs looked classy at first glance. Expensive. Like a Vegas club in a Hollywood movie. Look deeper, though, and you would remember where you were. That the dark drapes were covering cracked and crumbling walls, that the music was being pumped in off an iPod, and that the lights were kept dim to hide the girls' bruises.

At three in the morning, the place was just getting going. Men and a few women reclined on large sofas as they watched the latest imported dancing girls. They also gambled. And they snorted.

At least the sucking and fucking was conducted in private, out of view.

Bull led me to a dark corner near the bar and pushed me down into one of the sofas. As he walked away, I saw one of the dancers start to approach me with her money smile in place, but a glare from Bull made her stop in her tracks. Then I smelled a familiar perfume.

It was rich and musky, worn by a woman with a type of class none of the dancers could mimic. As Veronica Gaines walked across the room, everyone stopped for a moment to follow her with their eyes. Her suit was dark and sharp, to match her hair. Unlike the club, she didn't seem to be hiding any bad bits. She slid onto the sofa beside me and handed me an amber drink.

"Orange juice for me," I said, with a little too much force.

Gaines noted it with a slight smile. She nodded a signal at someone I couldn't see, and the juice appeared moments later on the table beside me.

"Eoin." Gaines said my name as though she liked it. "It's been awhile."

"You've got my number; you could have called. Or were you hoping to impress me by sending a driver?"

"You'd know if I wanted to impress you." She smiled again. "I mostly did it to annoy you."

"Well, it worked."

"How's your new flat? You moved out to Wednesbury, right?"
Subtext: I've still got you on-leash.

I just nodded and sipped my juice.

She looked me up and down. "How are you healing up?"

Subtext: Hope you feel well enough to work.

"It's fine. A few pills, you know."

"And how is the football going? Are any of our boys going to make it?"

Gaines, who had set up a youth club in the family name as a publicity stunt, had hired me to coach football to the local kids. It was outreach stuff, using football to bring together the different ethnic groups and to work with children the schools were giving up on. It was community work paid for with blood money, and the only job I'd ever enjoyed.

"I wouldn't hold out hope. I've got Bauser's kid brother involved now. He's got some game. But he's already too old for the scouts."

In sports, just like everywhere else, the decisions were made young.

Gaines pretended to think about what I'd said before getting to the point.

"There's somebody I want you to meet. He needs help, and I think you're just the man to give it."

"This doesn't sound like football coaching."

"I won't ruin the surprise. I've given him your mobile number, and he'll be in touch when the hours are more civil. It'll be interesting for you, working for someone who works during daylight. There's a whole world there, you know?"

"And what am I supposed to do?"

"I'll leave that for him to explain. It's perfect for you."

Darkness danced in her eyes. There was a joke I wasn't in on.

"No, thanks, I want to stick to the coaching."

"You'll be able to fit in both, don't worry about that."

"Listen, Ronny." I tried the nickname for effect, looking for a reaction. I didn't get one. "Last time I got involved in any of your business, my innards got cut and spliced. I'm out of that game."

Working for Gaines was the reason I'd been attacked. The situation had left four people dead and had made Gaines a lot of money. It made sense. Behind every hero is someone turning a profit.

She shrugged. "I'm sure we can throw enough of a pay raise at you to make you change your mind."

I was sure she could, too.

"So why couldn't this person just approach me himself?"

"He doesn't know about this meeting. But I want to impress upon you how important this is to us. *All of us.*"

"*All* of us?" I said, mimicking her serious tone. "Is this from your old man, or did you just develop a multiple personality?"

"When you need help, we'll be here," she said, her face anything but amused. She reached inside her suit jacket and produced a thick bundle of notes that somehow hadn't ruined the lines of her suit. "Your new client will want to pay you. He's honest like that. But you'll shrug it off, okay? Pretend you're doing it for free."

I sat there for a minute and tried to think of a moral high horse to climb up on. Then I took the money and stayed quiet. She eyed me up and down for a minute; then she nodded a dismissal.

As she stood up to leave, she paused and looked down at me.

"You *will* need our help. When the time comes, don't hesitate. And, Eoin? I mean it. This one needs doing."

No pressure.

She turned and walked away. The eyes followed her across the room again as she left. I felt the money in my hand, and I hoped, not for the first time, that whatever part of her was kept hidden away was something sad and lonely.

Some of the dancers saw the cash in my hand and began to circle.

THREE

I'll let you in on a secret.

There's no such thing as an honest client. Not for me. There's a whole world set up for honest people. They can go to the police or the newspapers. They can call the Citizens Advice Bureau. They have support groups. People who come to me are people with something to hide.

So it came as a shock to be contacted by a Catholic priest.

I'd made it to bed as the sun started to bleed its way across the morning sky. The light poured through the window and washed over me. It felt good. It had been a long, wet winter, and even the cold March sunlight felt like an improvement.

The phone woke me up shortly before noon.

"Is this Mr. Miller?"

I don't wake well. My response was half spoken, half grunted. He introduced himself, and over the course of an awkward conversation that was like being asked on a blind date, we arranged to meet at the church after closing. I had to ask what the open hours were.

Why would Gaines be paying me to help a priest? As the meeting time approached, I sat in the pub, clinging to an orange juice.

Running the numbers, thinking through the scams. Trying to see in what way this might possibly screw me. If I'd sat there another five minutes, I would have talked myself out of going.

Father David Connolly was waiting for me at the gate. He smiled and took my hand between both of his. They were large and warm, and it felt like he was holding my hand between two fleshy cricket gloves. The rest of him seemed too small in comparison. He looked around sixty, but not tired out; his eyes still seemed to have fire in them. He pointed in the direction of the church, and I walked on ahead of him. I settled into a pew near the front as he followed behind, locking us in. There is something very unsettling about a church at night; generations of ghosts sit at your shoulder.

"I'm not very comfortable with this," he said as he settled into the pew in front of me.

"If it helps," I said, "neither am I."

When he spoke, I caught the vaguest trace of an Irish brogue in his Midlands accent. He spoke quietly and chose his words carefully. It wasn't hard to picture him standing in front of a congregation, using the same slow cadence while reading passages from the Bible.

"I've never been hired by a priest before," I said. "You're not going to ask me to find God, are you?"

A smile played at his lips. "I know exactly where he is, don't worry."

Priests have a kind of earnestness that makes me nervous. I'm used to lies. I can trust them. Depend on them. Honesty scares the hell out of me. Faith? Even more menacing. It made me want to lash out.

"That's why you called the Gaines family?"

The comment hit him hard. There was a big bundle of something tender, and I'd hurt it. His flinch was visible.

"She told you?" He shrugged and then came out fighting. "I shouldn't be surprised. She's her father's daughter all right, always messing with people. Does the dirty work bother you?"

Both of us paused. We all write a book in our minds about the people we meet. I wondered for the second time what he was writing in mine. I was drawing on an anger I didn't understand. The story of my life: I never know when to use it and when to run.

"No," I said. "Honest work bothers me."

"Dirty or honest, I do need your help," he said. "I work with a lot of charity groups, as you can imagine. These days most of them are aimed at helping immigrants from the Middle East, or people who have fled war zones, Afghanistan and Libya."

"All of our greatest hits."

"Yes."

"Not that many Christians coming from there, though, surely?"

He bridled for a second, like he wanted to correct me, but then he let it go. "There's all kinds. But I know what you mean. Truth is, only a small part of the work I do is through the church these days. A lot of it is out of hours, so to speak. I know it's the cool thing to insult the Catholic Church, but we're still here to help people." He shrugged. "Right now, that usually means I take the collar off and talk to people as David, rather than Father David."

"Hope you get paid overtime."

He pointed up at the large cross behind the altar. The man stared down at us from beneath his crown of thorns, looking hurt and lonely. "There's a legend about a gypsy who…" He paused, unsure if he'd said something wrong. I nodded for him to go ahead. It was okay. The word *gypsy* only bothers me if a moron is using it. "Okay, then. Do you know it? The legend about gypsies making the nails?"

My father loved the old myths. They were part of his religious upbringing, and he came alive when he told them. I thought back to the way I'd first heard it from him.

"A gypsy was hired by a Roman soldier to make twelve nails, to be picked up the next day. That night, his daughter had a vision of what the nails would be used for. She managed to steal back all but three of them, which made the Romans angry. We've been on the run ever since."

He nodded. "With just God's love to protect you."

I tried not to laugh out loud.

"What am I here for, Father?"

His mouth opened and closed. His lips framed words, and then he gave up before he spoke. Eventually he stopped looking for the delicate and went straight for the honest.

"Rape."

FOUR

Just one word.

That was all it took to turn my world around. Words have power. I grew up being cut by them, reacting to them in pain or anger, at people who infused them with venom because they were scared of me.

Pikey.

Gyppo.

Scum.

Those slurs meant nothing to me now. I'd grown tough enough to shrug them off. Connolly had used one, though, that still came precharged.

He read my mind. "Yes. Years ago, I heard the confessions of a woman, a girl, who had been forced to…raped. She had been raped. I counseled her, comforted her. I said nothing to anybody. If you lock something like that up, if you don't speak out, you become a prisoner to it."

"You want me to find the guy?"

"No, he's long dead." He stared up at the cross for a second, lost in memories. "We all have some pain to carry, you know?"

Did I ever. I smiled and waited for him to continue.

"I've been doing this for a long time. Too long, maybe, I don't know. At my age it makes you think. What have I done? Really? Wearing the collar and doing Mass, that's not enough. That's just a job, but what difference have I made? You hear things you never wanted to. I've heard just about everything. But to be honest? There are some things I'm sick of hearing. Sick of carrying. Sick. I want to retire having gotten something done."

The way he hit the word *sick* made me wonder if there was something else going on. If it wasn't just his age that was wearing him down. We were interrupted by a gentle buzzing sound. It took me a few seconds to realize it was a doorbell. Churches have doorbells. Amazing.

"Ah, there she is." Connolly rose to his feet and hurried away. "There's someone else I wanted to join us. I'll be right back."

He was already out of sight as his last words reached me. I could hear him unlocking all the doors he'd locked after I'd arrived. Lots of banging as he moved heavy locks, and then a muffled greeting, followed by the banging again as the locks were put back in place.

Connolly walked back down the aisle, followed by a woman a few years younger than me. Clearly of Muslim extraction, she was dressed for an office job, and she had the "young professional" thing down pat. She looked familiar, although I couldn't place her.

"Eoin Miller, this is Salma Mina." Connolly introduced us as I stood up and held out my hand, almost embarrassed by the fact that I was trying to act like a gentleman.

We shook hands, and I became very aware that my hand smelled of ginger biscuits. When she spoke, her voice sounded as familiar as her name.

"I've heard a lot about you, Mr. Miller."

There was a slight edge to her voice. She'd obviously done her homework on me. It didn't take much digging to find dirt in my past. I said she could call me Eoin, and she smiled, but her guard stayed up, like a sheet of glass between us.

Her smile finally tipped me off: I'd seen her face on billboards around town. She was a local celebrity with a popular radio show, the flavor of the month in the regional media. Her local accent was stronger in person. Connolly motioned for us to sit. The pews hadn't been designed for a conference, and I had to twist round in a way that made my scarred insides hurt. I had some painkillers in my coat, but I left them untouched. I didn't like taking them in front of people.

The three of us exchanged looks for a second, and then Connolly coughed and spoke. "We run—well, Salma runs—a local community charity."

"Women's group?"

Salma shook her head, but it wasn't a fully committed denial. "No. It's a support group for immigrants. We've sort of started an old-fashioned community center: we help newcomers connect with people from their home country, provide them with work contacts, arrange events so they can mingle…"

She trailed off and looked to Connolly for support, clearly wanting help in finishing her description. He nodded. "We help them get settled in the area. It's mostly Muslim women, to be honest, but we do get some Poles and some Kurds. We help them get jobs, meet people. The ones from more traditional families, well, they have strong incentives to keep to their own, you know?"

"I would imagine it's not easy."

"We keep it as low-key as we can. We've managed to keep the story away from the media, so there's nothing for the right wing to dig into. But you're right, there are plenty of bigots out there who don't like the idea. They're not shy about it, either." There was a hard look in her eyes.

"I was talking about the families of these women. I imagine that not everyone is pleased by your offer to help."

"Oh. Well, yes. Some of the families don't like it, you're right." She shrugged. "Some people just want to be with their own, and that's fine. Some people find me too Western—they don't like the way I dress or talk—and I can understand that. Some don't like having David involved. We try and make it work."

They were talking to the wrong Miller. This was exactly the sort of stuff my little sister had turned into her life's work. She always talked about immigration and race relations like she was standing on a podium. Even in private conversation she acted like she was holding a microphone. *Look at me, look at how noble and right I am.*

But I wasn't my sister. I looked at the woman and the priest. I'd had enough nice talk.

"Okay. Now tell me what you've been working up to."

A church is the best place for an awkward silence. I'd never thought about it, but the stone floors and high ceilings really let the emptiness of the moment echo. Connolly and Salma shared a few glances before Connolly put the conversation back on track and answered my question.

"It started with a young Polish girl. Her family has been in England for years now, but they're still an active part of the group. She goes to the local high school. She came to me in tears one day, asking about—" He paused. When he spoke again, I saw a flicker of something in his eyes. "Pregnancy and abortion."

Salma took it up. "We both talked to her, tried to get her to go to the police or her parents, but she wouldn't. What happened changed her. She's a different girl now."

I'd seen that before. It reminded me of a song lyric—something about how you spend half your life covering up, waiting for the kick.

"I—well, there's always something else, you know? Paperwork, meetings, people who need something." Salma shook her head. "You keep pushing the problem back down under the pile, for when you have more time to deal with it. Then another girl changes."

"Did this second one talk to you?"

"No. She's from one of the more traditional families. This isn't something she'll talk about. We probably wouldn't have noticed it if we hadn't already seen the emotional withdrawal in the other girl first."

"Have you asked her?"

Connolly spoke. "If you can figure out a way to do it, please let us know."

Fair point.

"And then there was a third. This time, it was a girl from a Kurdish family that just came over from Turkey. Her mother knows, but they don't want to report it to the police."

"Why not?"

Connolly pulled a face. "Too many reasons to go into."

"What kind of reasons? This is what the police are for. You know who I am. I find thieves and runaways. I find stolen drug money. And yes, I work for the people who can't go to the police. But this?"

Connolly stood up in the aisle next to me and stretched his legs.

"Have you seen how the police handle rape cases? They don't even try, let alone get convictions. Even worse, how the press dives right in? It's a circus. And that's for white women. That's for people the public *likes*. I can only imagine the backlash if the victims were asylum seekers."

Salma spoke quietly, with a purpose that rocked me. "*We* don't trust them. Do you watch the news? Anytime some government official panics about terrorism, they drag everyone with dark skin and beards out into the street and put it on TV."

It was true. There had been a lot of damage done in the wake of the London bombings. I'd seen news broadcasts on TV talk shows where cops bundled Asians into the back of police vans at gunpoint, and at the press conference afterward, they didn't even bother to differentiate among Muslims, Sikhs, and Hindus. The men were nearly always released without charge; the Brazilian student who'd been shot dead simply for being the wrong shade of brown when he ran away from armed police had not been so lucky. So, it looked like Gaines had been right. The real police would be useless. This job had me written all over it.

"They don't know who's doing it? The girls, I mean?"

"No." Connolly shook his head. "Two of them talked to us, and neither knew the attacker. We think he was wearing a mask, but we haven't pressed them yet."

"What links the victims? Were they at the same meetings?"

"Yes. There's a youth group, an afterschool thing. All three of them are part of that. Or were, anyway, before this."

"Have you come across any hate groups? Heard of anyone out to get immigrants?"

Salma had come prepared for that question. She handed me a folded piece of paper. I opened it enough to see a brief list of names, and then I folded it again and put it in my pocket.

But even now that I had more details, there was one question I needed an answer to.

"Like I said, you know who I am. What is it you're wanting? What can I give you that the cops can't?"

When Connolly answered, it was with a coldness that hit me like a punch to the gut. "Stop the bastard."

I thought of Veronica Gaines at the club, her words to me.

When the time comes, don't hesitate.

FIVE

I had arranged to meet Terry Becker that evening to see the Wolves match. Becker was my best friend by default, and the only person who would sit through a football match with me. He was also the only guy who'd been stubborn enough to stand by me through every stupid decision that I'd ever made—which was saying something. Since he was still a cop, we had an unspoken agreement not to talk shop. It had been well over a year since I'd left the force, so we'd had plenty of time to work out our little dance. During the match, we managed it beautifully. But I blew it on the drive home.

"What would you say about a rape investigation where you couldn't get physical proof and the victim wasn't talking?"

"You're looking into a rape?"

Shrug. "I didn't say that."

"This Gaines-related?"

A lie, but only a small one. "No."

"Would you have proof that it happened?"

"No statement from the victim, no medical."

He shook his head and slowed down the car. "You mean no actual proof?"

I had to give him that point. I shrugged and said yes.

"Then there would be no case. CPS wouldn't touch it with a ten-foot pole, so neither would we."

"I thought that's what you'd say."

He pulled over and gave me the look, like we were five-year-olds and I'd just accused him of stealing my chocolate. "Don't say that, Eoin. You know what I mean."

"That you're not interested? Don't worry about it."

He let that go for a minute and stared ahead, his fingers drumming on the wheel. I thought he was going to leave it be and drive on, but he sighed and turned to face me.

"I see the stats on these things now. I know how it goes." Becker had swapped his job at CID for an analyst gig on a new intelligence unit, part of a reshuffle by the new commissioner. "Something like one in twenty rape cases goes to conviction. And that's *with* evidence. Rapes make the brass shit their pants, and when the people above you take a dump, guess where it falls? Nobody wants a piece of it."

"Then who could I take it to?"

He thought about it as he pulled the car back into traffic.

"Why not Laura?"

My sorta-wife. We were technically still married because the divorce paperwork never seemed to turn up. She'd been promoted to DCI ahead of time after taking credit for the same drug bust that had landed me in the hospital.

I shook my head.

"You said the brass wouldn't touch it, and she's brass now."

"Yeah," said Becker. "But she's—"

A woman.

I understood the unspoken words as if they'd appeared in a speech bubble. As we pulled up outside my flat, I gave Terry a chance to redeem himself.

"Hey, listen, did you know Ned's Atomic Dustbin have a gig coming up? At the Wulfrun, next Tuesday. Fancy it?"

He looked at me with a bored expression. "Eoin, I never went for that grebo shit when it was trendy. Why would I go for it now?"

Grebo. There was a word I hadn't heard in a long time. It had been a great music scene. Unless you liked cleanliness. Ned's was a group that was both loud and local. Becker had never been a fan of either of those qualities in music. In fact, one look at the CDs on his backseat could tell you he wasn't really a fan of music at all. More than once I'd caught him singing along to Coldplay on the radio.

"Come on, man, it'll be great."

"I'm sure. Have fun with that."

We sat in silence for a while before he tried again. "Look, Eoin, a person goes missing, you're good at finding them. If someone steals something or owes someone money, you're the guy. But this? Is this a Gaines thing?"

I stayed silent again. To deal with Becker was to deal with his inner five-year-old. Once you understood that, you were in control. Give him the silent treatment, and he caves.

"I'll see what I can do," he said, starting the engine.

I watched his taillights disappear before turning to my front door. Tomorrow, I would have to start looking for someone who didn't want to be found. I would need to ask for help from the last woman in the world who would want to give it to me. And I'd have to win the trust of a group of strangers who wouldn't want to confide in me. Maybe this was my chance. I'd heard that anyone who could pull off three miracles could officially be declared a saint.

But first I needed to try to get some sleep.

My flat was above a photography studio in Wednesbury, seven miles outside Wolverhampton. I'd thought moving out of the city would get me away from all the bad memories of a failed job and marriage, but I was finding out memories tend to stay with you wherever you go. The flat had two bedrooms, two floors, and a brand-new shiny kitchen. What it wasn't supposed to have was a pissed-off-looking man with a cricket bat.

I saw him as soon as I switched the light on in the hallway. He had dragged one of my cheap armchairs into the middle of the living room so that he would be facing the front door when I walked in. The cricket bat leaned against the side of the chair. He didn't move to touch it, but his hand rested near its handle so the threat was clear. He was in his early forties and dressed immaculately in a charcoal suit. His fingers were covered with rings that gleamed almost as much as his balding head. His goatee was a darker shade than the rest of his hair, an obvious dye job.

If I hadn't known better, I would have taken him for any number of small-time local businessmen, first-generation immigrants from Pakistan or India. But unfortunately I did know better. This was Channy Mann, the other side of Wolverhampton's criminal cold war. And I had been responsible for the death of his little brother.

I doubted this was a social call.

SIX

I stood in silence. He sat in the chair and grinned like a cat that had just swallowed a bird whole. After beating it to death with a cricket bat.

"Um…can I get you a coffee?"

I wanted to get into the kitchen where the knives were. I have good, sharp knives.

"I've already made it." He pointed to my coffee table, where two mugs were giving off steam.

"Milk? Sugar? I have both if you—"

"Miller, get in here."

I took the final cautious steps required to reach my living room. As ordered. Once there, Channy's air of menace dropped away. He beamed and stood up, taking my hand in a strong welcoming grip between both of his.

"Man, it's been awhile, hasn't it?"

"Yeah, it's been, what, five months? Ever since—" Way to go. Bring up the dead brother. Miller, you are a star.

"Yes, ever since Gaurav was taken from us." He shook his head slowly. He looked me dead in the eye as he continued. "But at least they caught the bastard who did it, eh?"

Was he testing me, or was I testing him? The man convicted of killing Gav Mann was innocent. Well, innocent of that crime, anyway. He'd committed plenty others. I'd gone from working for Channy and his brother to working for the opposing team. He had to know I was involved. His grip tightened, and he pulled me in closer. His grin twisted into something nasty, and it was wide enough for me to see his missing molars.

"We both know who killed my brother, eh?"

I pulled away as politely as possible and tried to stay calm. My heart was beating far harder than the smell of coffee would give it reason to. I glanced around the room, trying not to make it obvious that I was looking for something to pick up. I had a Les Paul Junior guitar in the corner. I had made a few unsuccessful attempts at learning the folk and punk songs that my mother had sung to me as a child. I knew it had a nice heavy weight to it. I just had to get there.

"That Gaines cunt." He spat the words out. "She walks around with her protection, thinks she can take the whole fuckin' town. She's never had to step up. She wouldn't know how. My day? We had to prove it first. If you couldn't hit, you couldn't talk. You didn't get a say."

I nodded. Looked encouraging. Please, go on. Keep talking and don't kill me.

He was working up a full rant now. He put his hand on my shoulder. "She just walks around like she's on *The Apprentice* or something, like this shit we're into is something for fucking corporate suits. The whole world, man, the whole world is run by accountants and cunts now."

Channy's language surprised me. I'd never heard him swear before, not even once. He'd always been the calm brother, the political one. There had even been a time when he'd looked set to go into local politics, but the guys in power hadn't wanted another criminal. Politics in Black Country was a racket of its own, full of doublespeak and special handshakes. So the council had "encouraged" him not to run and had given him permission for all his building projects. As long as he didn't want a seat at the table, he could run the rest of the restaurant.

"We need to take her out." He saw me catch the use of the word *we*. His smile almost winked at me. "Yeah. You're in this with me, too. Man, just because you sold that house of yours doesn't mean you can forget who paid for it."

"I guess not."

Sometimes there's just no way out from under, is there?

"I know Gaurav was on his way to meet you when they got him. So you have a choice, Gyp. It's your blood or hers."

Shit.

Moving far quicker than he had any right to, he seized the cricket bat with his hand and smashed both mugs with a fluid stroke. Black liquid erupted as the ceramic shattered and coffee splashed, still steaming, across my sofa and carpet. But I had other things to worry about. He stroked the bat again, and this time my armchair fell forward and hit the floor with a sickening thump. It was missing a leg. He was next to me now, making one final stroke clearly destined for my kneecap. I saw the bulge of large muscles against his suit jacket as he bought the bat to an instant stop just before the point of impact. I almost dropped the contents of my bladder right there. He ran the bat up the outside of my thigh gently, until it was pressing into my waist.

"You work for her now, maybe. But you still work for me. She can't have her guards all the time—nobody can. You're going to find a moment when she's alone, when she don't look so tough, and you're going to call me, yeah?"

He put pressure on the bat, and I said yes.

"Good. Now clean this fuckin' place up, you pig."

He brushed past me and left. I stared at the wreckage in my living room. Channy was right about one thing. This would take a lot of cleaning up.

SEVEN

Every day that you wake up with full use of your kneecaps should be a celebration of life. I celebrated with a bacon sandwich. Not just any bacon sandwich—this one was lightly fried in some garlic and pepper, with melted cheese over the top.

I scanned the list Salma had given me and recognized a few names, mostly guys who had been bullies back when I'd been at school. As far as I knew, these types would still be found in their local pubs, collecting their unemployment and working on liver damage.

Could one of them force himself onto a woman? I didn't find that hard to believe. Would any of them have what it took to run a serious hate campaign against immigrants? No way.

But there was another name that interested me: the People's Community Party, or PCP. Originally, it had been called the English Socialist Party, or ESP. I'd policed one of their rallies toward the end of my time in uniform, and they hadn't made me especially welcome. Hanging around angry skinheads waving Union flags and shouting racist chants isn't my idea of fun. Everyone knew they'd been involved in a riot in Dudley over plans to build a new mosque, but nobody could prove it. Their negative media profile had been enough to warrant a rebrand. Like changing a chocolate bar's packaging or selling "New Coke," the party leaders had ditched the ESP title in favor of the newer, more inclusive People's Community Party. I guessed they hadn't noticed that shortened to PCP until they'd already ordered all the business stationary. Their posters were all over town in preparation for the local elections in May. A good showing there would give them momentum going into the national elections. If the PCP made big gains in the Midlands, of all places, then the rest of Britain would have to take note. This could get interesting.

First I had to get to my day job.

I got to the sports hall early. The place had been built the previous year, a community project for the surrounding estates, a chance to get involved and play sports. It made a nice story for the papers. What the media didn't seem to talk about was that the Gaines family had footed the bill. Another sports hall was being built on the heath town estate across town. I'd already agreed to work there, too.

It was a freestanding building, modeled on the sports halls springing up at local high schools. A small monument to concrete and paint. Most of the interior was given to the playing area itself, but there was a changing room, a storage room, and a seated balcony area for spectators. Sometimes the parents of the children would sit and watch; sometimes it was scouts from the local football clubs.

I folded out the five-a-side goals and laid out the cones for the warm-up drills. I tested the pressure of the footballs and played by myself for a while, living out a few adolescent dreams of scoring great goals in important games.

The first few kids arrived straight from school, their voices announcing them long before they turned up. I sent them straight into the locker room to get changed, and then I held back a smile as they came out dressed to play and started acting out the same fantasy moments I'd been running through myself moments earlier.

Raj, a fourteen-year-old Hindu with a deft touch and a loud mouth, commentated on his own genius as he ran past. "He takes it past one…oh, and another. Nutmeg. This guy is on fire."

I put my foot on the ball, killing the play and sending Raj tumbling from his own momentum. Everyone else laughed, and Raj climbed to his feet even more determined to score that great goal. He got the ball from me and then jinked past his friends and kicked the ball into the goal. Okay, there was no goalkeeper, but that wasn't the point. He did a circuit of the hall, celebrating to an imaginary crowd. He shut up when the older boys arrived, already dressed in their football gear and ready to start. Raj was quieter when they were around.

I lined them all up and did the roll call, and I noticed the few who were missing. Then I got them started on their warm-up. I made them do two laps of the hall and then run between the cones I had laid out. They were quiet to begin with, focusing on the running, but soon their tongues loosened and the jokes started. They mentioned the size of one another's dicks as often as they mentioned their names. There was lots of hand slapping and talk of girls.

I pulled Raj to one side and told him he'd done well earlier.

"What you mean?"

"I made you look a fool, but you didn't lash out. You put your head down, got the ball back, and proved your point the right way. When you first came in here a couple months ago, you would have shinned me."

"Yeah, well. I don't need to. I'm a better player than you, no?"

He laughed and joined back in with the running. He was learning how to hold himself. Soon he'd be confident enough to clown around in front of the older kids. As the kids were finishing the warm-up, Marcus Boswell tried to sneak in behind me.

"Nice of you to join us, Boz."

He smiled sheepishly. "Sorry, Gyp. Mom wanted me to go home first. You know how she is."

I did. The last time I'd seen her had been at the funeral for Boz's older brother, Bauser, a stopper for the Mann brothers. I'd pushed the guy for information, caught him up in my business, and that had gotten him killed. I wanted to keep Boz on the right track. He was the great hope of the team, too. He was still young enough that Wolves scouts were keeping half an eye on him. He was years behind their academy students, who were *really* learning to play football, but if I could get him fit and focused, they might give him a try. I wasn't going to let him have it easy, though.

"I don't care, Boz. You know the rules. Give me ten."

He rolled his eyes but didn't argue. He started doing laps of the hall while I divided everyone else into two teams and got a game started. When one kid kept up with some tackles that were too rough, I stopped play to ask him why.

"Cause I couldn't get the ball, man."

"So you couldn't get the ball. Just learn from it. Watch what the other guy did to keep the ball away from you, and then come up with a way to beat him next time. By the rules."

I blew the whistle during buildup play, happy to see the kids stop where they were and look around curiously. What came next was my way of teaching: we'd look at how the play was spread out and debate what the kid in possession should do next. Who should he pass to, and why? Where was the best space to play into?

Boz slotted straight into the game after his punishment and scored three goals in quick succession. He kept goading Raj, but it was good-natured. He was trying to get Raj to come out of his shell, and sometimes it worked. After the game I had them do a lap around the outside of the building and then talked them through some cool-down stretches. I almost managed to make it sound like I knew what I was talking about.

As they meandered off to the changing room, creating their own soundtrack of loud jokes and squeaking running shoes, I started packing away the equipment. Each kid called bye to me as he came out of the changing room and headed out the door. Boz was last, and he seemed to want to sneak out the same way he'd tried sneaking in.

"You okay, Boz?"

"Yeah, why?"

I cocked my head to one side.

"Because I know you, cob, and you're *not* okay."

He shrugged and turned to leave. He waved at me over his shoulder. I shook my head and decided to leave him alone. He knew where I was if he needed me. I was folding away the goalposts when I heard a powerful car start up outside. I made it out in time to see a black four-wheel-drive vehicle pulling out of the car park. Boz was sitting in the passenger seat. Behind the wheel was Letisha. I knew her. She was one of Channy Mann's lieutenants.

I swore out loud. I was losing him like I'd lost his brother.

In the changing room I checked my phone. There were seven missed calls and a voice mail. I recognized the number straightaway: Laura. My sorta-wife. The message was short but not sweet.

"Eoin, your mother's been taken to hospital. Call me. Now."

My mother? When I called back, it rang so long that I thought it would go to voice mail, but eventually she answered.

"It's about time," she said.

Under any other circumstances, I would never have passed up the chance to annoy her.

"What's happened?"

"She had a fall."

"Fall?"

Having a fall is what happens to old people. People who can't look after themselves and need help at home. People with arthritis. People with angina. People who fought in wars. It is not something that happens to *my* mother. A healthy woman in her fifties does not *have a fall*.

"Eoin, have you seen her lately?"

I tried to think of the last time I'd visited. It made me feel very small.

"Is she okay?"

Laura didn't answer. There was just the hiss of the phone connection and background noise of a hospital.

"Laura?"

"Look, I'm not a doctor. Just get over here, okay?"

"Which hospital?"

"Manor."

That was in Walsall, a couple towns over. Laura hung up. I stared at the phone for a minute.

The phone was shaking.

My hand was shaking.

When did everybody get so old?

The flames are dying out.

The water puddles around my feet. The fireman looks down at me and smiles.

"Don't worry, sunshine," he says, "we saved the booze."

We're stood outside my parents' pub. It's three in the morning, and I'm nine years old. This isn't the first time the place has burned.

One of the firemen puts his helmet on my sister's head, and she giggles.

My father walks among the firemen, thanking them. They will be expecting free drinks later, once their shifts have ended. Free drinks and maybe some sandwiches, because they will have noticed that the fire didn't touch the kitchen.

My father looks old. His shoulders sag.

My mother doesn't sing us any songs. She wraps the three of us in a big hug and smiles.

"Back to bed soon, don't worry."

She goes to talk to my father, putting a hand on his shoulder. They stand there for a moment, framed by the last wisps of smoke. It's the first time I see my parents look old. The first time I see my parents look fragile. I look into my brother's eyes and know he's seen it too.

EIGHT

All hospitals are made up of the same sounds and smells, but each one has a defining characteristic. The Manor hospital was lonely. It wasn't dilapidated or even empty, but it somehow felt forgotten. The sound of my feet squeaking on the floor echoed down the empty corridors as I made my way to the ward. My mother was in a room on her own. The only times I'd ever seen anybody in one of those solo rooms was because they were either rich or dying.

Laura was leaning against the wall outside, sipping from a plastic cup of coffee and staring as the steam rose from the top. She straightened up when she saw me coming, and almost offered a smile. She was looking good; being promoted clearly suited her. Stepping up to her new job had given her a little bit more of everything; she seemed a little taller and a lot stronger. She was born again. I knew what lengths she'd gone to gain this new authority, but neither of us wanted to talk about that.

"Relax," she said when I asked about the room. "Being married to a DCI has its privileges. At least it does for your mum."

"How is she?"

"She's asleep. She'll be okay, the doctor says. But she's shaken."

"How come you're here?"

"You're welcome."

I checked my ego for a moment. I smiled at Laura, and she smiled back. Just a little bit. "Sorry, I didn't mean it like that. Why did she call you and not me?"

"I'm her emergency contact at the moment."

That hurt. It probably showed. Three children and yet she chose her estranged daughter-in-law. Laura kept talking to try and cover any emotion, for the both of us.

"I've called your brother and sister, too. They're on their way."

"Great, a family reunion. We should probably start a campfire in the reception and make sure there's space for all the caravans in the car park."

She laughed and eased back against the wall. We'd often made jokes about my family over the years. She never meant any of them, and I meant only half of them. I wondered how she's tracked down my siblings. Last I'd heard my sister was living in Glasgow. I was clueless as to where. My brother? No idea. Laid out in a ditch somewhere from too much booze and gambling. Laura had obviously kept better track of them than I did. It was easy for her. Everyone liked Laura.

"What happened?"

"I told you—"

"How?"

"I don't know. She hasn't gone into any detail."

I put my hand onto the door handle. Before I pushed my way inside, Laura put her hand on my arm.

"Don't react," she said.

I walked into the room and took a long look at my mother. She looked old. She was dozing with the television on mute, the channel tuned to a daytime soap. I walked round the bed to sit by her side. Her arm was bandaged, and the way she was positioned seemed to favor one hip. I carefully avoided her face. It's the first place you notice any age or weakness in the people you care about.

The last place you want to look, sometimes. When I did look, it wasn't the age or the weakness that I noticed.

It was the blossoming black eye.

A swelling spread outward from her eye, threatening to merge with another bruise on her cheek. I knew this kind of bruise. It wasn't the kind caused by any fall; these were deliberate.

I'd seen this woman stand up to the police, to bailiffs, and to people who would burn down her family's home. I'd never seen her take a beating.

Laura stood in the doorway. She caught the expression in my eyes and nodded for me to join her outside.

"Who did this?"

She made to put her hand on my arm again, but I shrugged it off.

"Laura—"

"I don't know."

"What—"

"Look, all we know is what she told us. She says she had a fall. She says she doesn't want to cause a fuss. I've seen the same things as you, and I've called in some favors to get the situation looked at. But, Eoin, if she doesn't want to cause a fuss—"

I killed it with a look. My mother had never shied away from causing a fuss in her life. It was due to her stubbornness that I had been raised in the settled life. It had cost her a marriage, eventually, but she'd fought every step for her children to have a home and go to one school, to have the same things other children had. The things we wouldn't have had if we were shunted from camp to camp by the local councils.

And now someone had hit her.

"Channy. He came to see me last night, did a little redecorating with a cricket bat."

Laura leaned in and looked me over, as if expecting to see bruises. She asked if I was okay.

"Fine. He didn't do anything to me, but my carpet looks like it was roughed up by a really pissed-off barista. Now this—"

She shook her head.

"Gav Mann, maybe, but this has never been Channy's style. What would he have to gain? He already threatened you. He's made his point."

"Where did she 'fall'?" We both knew at this point it was just a euphemism for something else.

Laura seemed to debate whether to answer. She knew why I was asking. She knew she had a duty to her job. She also had no moral high ground when it came to breaking the law.

"At her house."

I smiled at her.

"Thanks for looking after her," I said. "Say hi to my family for me."

I walked away down the corridor, trying not to burst into a run. Time to visit my mother's house.

See? I'm not such a bad son.

NINE

I kept an eye out as I drove down my mother's street. It was quiet and residential. Nobody who lived there was rich, but they all took pride in their small kingdoms. Quiet, safe, and mortgaged to the hilt. The semidetached houses had been built at the start of the last century and withstood two world wars and countless recessions. There was a church at the bottom of the road that had been flattened by a German bomb during an air raid, but not one single house in the street had fallen down. You could raise a family here and teach them that the fullness of their ambitions needn't stretch beyond the end of the street.

There was a police car parked halfway down, and I saw a couple of uniforms chatting to someone in a doorway. Since my mother was not reporting the crime, there wouldn't be an official investigation. Laura had clearly pulled in some favors to get a few guys down here. I eased the car to the curb in front of my mother's house, most of it hidden from the road by a tidy privet hedge.

The only person I still knew who lived on the street, aside from my mother, was Mrs. Daniels. She lived across the road, and I'd helped her with a few DIY jobs over the years. I crossed the street, pushed through her gate, and rang the bell. It took her so long to answer the door that I might as well have taken a run round the block.

"Eoin," she said when she opened the door.

She gave me the full false-teeth smile, shining and awkward.

"Hiya, Mrs. D. How are you?"

"Oh, I'm fine. But listen, how's Erica? I've been so worried."

"You saw them take her away?"

"Oh yes. She was all wrapped up and on one of those boards. It looked like a car accident."

"She's going to be okay. She's a bit banged up. She'll still insist on mowing your lawn for you, I'm sure."

She made as if to invite me in for a cup of tea, but I said I couldn't stay.

"Did you see what happened?"

"Oh no. I was just telling your friends"— she meant the police; she still had it in her head that I worked for them—"that the first I knew was when the ambulance came roaring down the street. Your Laura came too. In fact, I'm sure she was here before the ambulance."

"Have you seen anyone visiting Mum today?"

"There was that man she doesn't like. I can't remember his name, but he's been round a lot lately. He was here this morning."

"What does he look like?"

"Oh, you know, he's just a bad one, him. Has that look about him."

"Was he wearing a coat? A hat? Got any hair?"

"Yes, I'm sure he has."

"Was he white? Asian?"

"Oh, he's white, all right. I think. Looks the sort, you know?"

I pretended to know what that meant and told her to get in out of the cold. I crossed the road and let myself into my mother's house with my spare key.

That man she doesn't like.

I had no idea who that was.

I found a mess in the living room. A potted plant was on its side, dirt spilling out. A plate had been smashed, as though it had hit the wall with some force. A cup lay empty on the floor. It smelled like coffee and something else that I couldn't put my finger on.

My mother hates coffee.

Who was here drinking it? I heard the sound of the cat flap, and seconds later a small ginger blur was doing laps around my legs.

The cat, Rollo.

"Some help you were."

I knelt down to give him some fuss. He purred a response, not sounding the least bit guilty, the little fucker. He followed me into the kitchen, where I dug out a pouch of cat food and slopped it into a dish for him.

"She better get out soon," I said, "because I'm not looking after you."

He seemed to look at me quizzically before he returned to his food. On my way out of the kitchen, I noticed something on the door that led to the living room: a patch of badly cracked paintwork and dented wood. I'd seen something like that before, investigating a case in which an attacker had repeatedly rammed a victim's head into a cupboard door. My stomach turned over and began to burn. To calm myself down, I cleared the mess.

After sweeping up the smashed crockery and doing the once-round with the Hoover, the room was as clean as I'd ever seen it. Rollo supervised and even seemed to approve. By the front door, I looked through the mail. It was the usual pile of circulars, free newspapers, bills, and bank statements. There were five or six manila envelopes with the same return address. I opened one, and then a second. By the time I reached the fourth, I knew what the fifth one would hold. They were all financial demands. It looked like my mother owed a large sum of money to a company called Kyng & Bootle. The letter was signed by David Kyng.

I could easily imagine the type of company these letters were coming from. My family had never had a credit rating. I'd never asked where my father had gotten the money for the pub, but it wouldn't have been a loan or a mortgage; he went through less official channels. Buying the house had only been an option because our family had gotten insurance money when we'd been burned out of the pub. The mainstream world had never been very welcoming to the Roma and still weren't, after all these years. That's how our kind ended up dealing with places like Kyng & Bootle, which handed out loans to people with credit problems. They preyed on desperation and panic. I didn't want to put too much thought into why my mother had gone begging to these people. But they wanted her to pay up now; that was for sure. The most recent demand was dated four days earlier. It promised a home visit from one of their collections agents. The address at the top of the page was listed as Broad Street, in Wolverhampton. The Gaines family owned most of the buildings on that street, and I decided that it was time for Kyng & Bootle to take a turn receiving a visitor.

I pocketed one of the letters and looked through the bank statements. All the mortgage payments were going out on time. Why did she need such a large sum of money from a loan shark?

I scanned the free paper and spotted a story on the front that was all about the PCP. The party was holding a rally that evening in Bilston, and its high-profile leader was going to be there. I checked the time and realized I could still just about make it. Kyng & Bootle would have to wait until business hours, anyway. In the meantime, I could distract myself with some paid work. Rollo stuck his head round the living room door as I put my coat back on.

"Seeya, creep," I said.

I swear the cat gave me the finger.

TEN

I headed to Bilston, which was another small town on the road to
the city. Some people still wouldn't call Wolverhampton "the city,"
but that's how I thought of it. It was still torn between the two
identities, though: by day it was a large town, and by night it was
a small city. It was no accident that the PCP was doing so much of
its campaigning in the Black Country. Some regions come in and
out of fashion in the national media, but the Black Country was
always ignored. Consisting of a large urban sprawl loosely connecting West Bromwich and Dudley to Wolverhampton, it was
full of struggling and disenfranchised working-class families.
Most politicians didn't speak for the people here. Football teams
like the Wolves and Albion were the only thing that drew the
string of local towns together, but that didn't connect the region
to the national media, which disregarded even the local football
teams. Political parties like the PCP could come in and say, "We're
here for you," and locals would take interest. Especially now that
the PCP was downplaying its racist and extremist policies, and
acting like its only focus was the economy and local problems, it

was possible it could trick people into supporting the party. It was certainly trying.

I drove into Bilston and pulled over near the town hall. It was one of those grand old beautifully crafted buildings with loads of history that completely lacked a modern purpose. Millions of pounds had been spent renovating it. The challenge had been finding a use for it. The PCP now paid rent there so at least some of the space was put to use, if not "good" use: the party had set up shop in one of the interior offices and used the hall for rallies and public events.

In the reception area an aged security guard looked up from his newspaper long enough to point me to the right doorway, which wasn't really necessary as it was the only suite in use that evening. At the doorway I found another reception area had been made. This one was makeshift, consisting of a small table stacked with piles of pamphlets and photographs. The main impression I got from looking at the literature was that this was an event that involved white men in suits wearing blue ties. The pamphlets were asking for votes and donations while promising little more than the hint of a firm handshake. The photographs were of families and celebrities but all had the same man at their center: a square-jawed man in his forties who could only be described as a poor man's JFK with an easy smile and a sharp suit. I remembered the man because he'd been the keynote speaker at the rally I'd policed; he'd been the only one who hadn't stirred the crowd into an angry mob.

A woman smiled up at me from the table. She looked to be in her forties. She wasn't fat, but she would be dependable in a windstorm.

"Hiya." She beamed at me.

Perfect teeth were framed by bright lipstick. Her eyes locked onto me like the headlights of an oncoming car. This moment would be interesting. So much had changed since I was a child. Back then my sallow complexion and shadowed eyes had stood out as foreign, but a generation of immigration from Eastern

Europe and the Balkans now meant many Roma didn't stand out that much from "normal" white people. Of course, every now and then someone would spot something different about me. I have *that look* about me. This time, though, I passed the test. There was no change in the way she looked at me. No sizing me up or narrowing of the eyes. I was white and proud.

I shook her hand to confirm it.

"Hi. I'd like to sign up."

"That's fine, dear. We just ask that you put your details on this form here." She passed me an official-looking paper. It asked my name, date of birth, address, occupation, ethnic origin, and who I last voted for. Was that even legal? It also asked what I felt would be the most important issues in the upcoming election, and it offered a selection to choose from plus a helpful section where I could get creative entitled "other."

I started filling in the form, lying in all the right places, and spelled my first name as "Owen" so that she wouldn't think I was Irish either.

"Busy tonight?" I asked as I wrote.

"Oh yes. Good turnout so far. It's going to be a good speech, I think. Rick's really been working hard on it."

"Rick?"

"Rick Marshall."

"Oh, right, yeah. Sorry. Mind's not switched on tonight." I knew Marshall's name. He had a national profile, and he represented the progress the party had been making. He'd defected to the PCP from the Conservatives after the last election and had taken the lead in reforming the party's image. If he was on the local campaign, it showed how important the result was to them.

"I know how it is. Long day, I take it?"

"The longest." I rolled my eyes in disgust at an imaginary day that involved boring meetings and a low-fat lunch instead of a local drug lord threatening me with a cricket bat and my mother being cruelly attacked. "Not a minute's peace."

"Well, it's good to see you still putting in the effort tonight. We do appreciate the support."

"You guys are saying what everyone else is scared to say, you know?"

"Thank you. Well, we like to think so. Everyone's gone PC-mad these days."

"Tell me about it. I got talking to a friend in the pub the other night, and he told me all about you guys, and I'm behind you all the way."

"We can always use more volunteers. What do you do for a living, Mr.—?"

"Miller, Eoin Miller. I'm between jobs at the moment. Seems every time I go for an interview it goes to someone less qualified."

She fixed me with a look of motherly concern and shook her head.

"The country's in a shocking state, isn't it? So many nice young men come in here and tell us the same thing. I tell you what, stick around after the talk and I'll introduce you to some of our team. We'll see what we can do."

I didn't even get a chance to say thank you. As soon as she finished the sentence, her eyes locked onto the person behind me in the queue. Clearly dismissed, I turned and walked past her table and into the main hall.

The hall was large and a little too warm. The noise of the crowd bounced between the shiny hardwood floors and the high ceilings. Every age range seemed to be represented, from pensioners to children who had been dragged along by their parents. I noticed a couple of camera crews from local TV news channels and some photographers from the regional newspapers. I recognized one of them as the guy who had taken pictures of me in the hospital after I'd been stabbed. Some of the news stories had played me up as a hero and an ex-cop; others had focused on my dirty past and gangland connections. I couldn't remember which angle his paper had taken, so I kept my distance. He noticed my arrival. If he was surprised to see me, he didn't show it.

There was a small catering table. It was behind a rope barrier, and I guessed it was for VIPs only because they had biscuits. I skirted the edge of the barrier to the entrance and, with nobody to stop me, wandered into the VIP area, trying to look as though I wasn't headed straight for the food. The orange juice was good. The biscuits were stale.

"I know." A friendly voice was followed by a soft slap on the shoulder. "They're awful, aren't they?" I turned to see the man from the pamphlets, Rick Marshall. "I don't know where Gladys gets them. Every event, it's the same selection. Would it kill her to get in some Jammie Dodgers?"

I choked back the mouthful of biscuit and took the hand he offered. The shake was as firm as the pictures suggested. I suddenly felt like the only person in the room and his new best friend.

"Rick Marshall," he said. "Mr.—?"

"Miller. Eoin Miller."

I saw the flash of something. He'd heard the name. It didn't have its usual effect, though. His eyes didn't narrow. He still held me locked in his gaze.

"Ah yes. The newspapers. You helped catch that killer awhile back, right?"

"I, uh, yes. I was good enough to bleed all over him until the police came. That threw him off, you know?"

He laughed. It was warm and infectious.

"Well, I'm sure you're downplaying your role there. It's a pleasure to meet you. Didn't I read that you were once in the force yourself?"

"Yes. For a while. I wasn't very good at it, but I did police one of your old rallies, when your party was still the ESP."

He tilted his head to one side and stepped closer, as though about to let me in on a secret. "National Socialism, who wants to be seen belonging to that tradition, right? It took a lot of work to get rid of them. Too many people saw the Union flag as an excuse to curse and fight, you know what I'm saying?"

"So you changed the name and the idiots went away?"

"No, I changed the name and then moved the party away from the idiots. It took a long time. But I think the opinion polls show it was worth it."

I looked round the room again. There wasn't a Union flag in sight. There were none of the symbols I'd come to associate with nationalism. He started speaking again, and I was surprised by the way my attention snapped right back to him. The guy was good.

I tried to rattle him. "And naming your party after a drug? Wise move. Everyone loves drugs."

"Yes, that was a bit of an oversight. But nobody really makes the connection. I like the name, especially the *community* bit. I'd wanted us to run with that on its own; it gives off the right vibes. Like a gated community, a symbol of safety."

"Depends which side of the gate you're on."

"You're not here to support the rally, are you?"

I thought about the things I'd planned to say. Then I thought, *Fuck it.*

"No flies on you. To be honest, no, I'm not one of your voters."

He nodded for a moment and then showed a little more of his hand, the cards he was holding back. "And you work for Veronica Gaines, right? Is she here? I'd love to talk to her."

"No, I'm here on my own time."

"Well, mention me to her, maybe? I'd love to run some of my ideas past her. With the elections less than two months away now, PCP is the place to be." One of his aides came and touched him on the shoulder. It was time for him to move on and become best friends with someone else. "I'm sorry, Eoin, but I have to get ready for my speech. I'd love to hear your thoughts on it afterward."

I watched him walk away through the crowd. I saw a round man with slicked-back hair step up to him and shake Marshall's hand. Marshall laughed off whatever was said and continued making his way across the room.

I listened to the start of his speech. It was all very stirring and civil. In fact, Marshall sounded just like every other politician I'd ever heard. He talked of taxes and schools and getting back to family values. When he got to the nationalism issue, he talked of progressive politics and asked the crowd why we had let the Far Right take hold of our most important symbols, like the British flag. I stopped listening: they'd never felt like my symbols to begin with. As I turned to leave, I saw the fat man again, flanked by two tall, muscular men wearing tattoos as though they were clothes. He was staring at me and whispering something to one of the guys.

I slipped out into the evening air and drove home. I popped a couple of pills to ease the pain in my stomach. My mind was blank on the drive; I don't think a single thought passed through it until I turned onto the car park outside my flat. As I climbed the stairs that led to my front door, I heard voices from inside and saw light coming from beneath the door. Someone was in my flat. *Again.*

I jangled the key in the lock as I turned it, making as much noise as I could. I pushed open the door.

"Whoever you are," I said as I stepped into the hallway, "you better have a damn good reason."

"Do I need a reason?"

Veronica Gaines was sitting on my sofa.

With my brother.

ELEVEN

This was a different Veronica Gaines from the one I was used to. She was dressed casually in jeans and a black shirt. She was drinking a glass of wine, and the smell of cooking was coming from the kitchen. My kitchen.

"Sorry," said Veronica, not looking sorry at all. "I always forget that it's not polite to let myself in to other people's homes. Bad habit, but let's be fair—it's not the worst one I've got."

The next thing I noticed was that my living room was clean. The stains from Channy's visit were gone, leaving just a slightly dark damp patch on the carpet and wall where someone had scrubbed.

"You know," she started again, "this place was a real tip. It's a nice flat. But really, Eoin, you should clean up after you have guests. I had to get someone in here to straighten the place out before we could even start dinner."

That hung in the air.

Guests?

"Hey, Smudge."

I knew it would take a few minutes for me to respond my older brother's greeting. I hadn't seen Noah in years. The last time was at my wedding, where he'd threatened to kill me. The time before that had been the other way around, and my hands had been on his throat. He was lounging on the sofa next to Veronica, his face leathery and hard-worn in comparison to her softer features. His dark hair was longish and sloppy, and his goatee showed a few patches of gray. He was dressed in flared jeans that looked like they'd been teleported from the seventies and a bright red shirt beneath a waistcoat. He had a crucifix hanging from his neck and wore too many bracelets for me to count. He couldn't have looked more like one of the Rolling Stones if he'd tried.

"Smudge?" Gaines turned to me with her eyebrow shooting for the heavens.

"It was the name our dai came up with for him when he was young," said Noah. "Eoin could find a patch of dirt wherever we went. He always found a way to get smudged."

Gaines laughed. I tried to get my feet under me and shake off the surprise that was making me feel so off-kilter. I tried to ask Noah what he was doing here, how he got in, and where he had been for four years. It all came out as a shake of my head.

"It's nice to see family, but it's not right to visit without looking up old friends, right?"

He sat up a little, nudged Gaines. Then he smiled at me, all innocent, as though what he'd said had no implications.

"Old friends? You two know each other?"

Gaines ignored my question. "He's been telling me stories about your history. Your people, I mean."

Noah could talk for hours about the past. Slavery. The Holocaust. India. Misery's greatest hits in the gypsy playbook. I hoped he'd stopped short of trying to convince her we were the lost tribe from the Bible. He stood up, and for a worrying moment I thought he was going to hug me. Instead he just slapped my arm. *Chara. Sar-Shen?*

We'd learned bits and pieces of the language when we were children, a secret code between us and our father that nobody else was in on.

"I'm doing okay."

"*Pandj besha, caco?*"

"*Chatchi.*"

He looked at Gaines and then at me, his grin still in place. "*Kur Gawdji?*"

"*Na. Singorus.*" I watched Gaines squirm, trying to hide her paranoia. It felt good. "*Otchi da drav.*"

Noah laughed. "*Perras, auli?*"

I decided it was time to stop acting like children. "*Rokker* English, *chara?*"

"Sorry." Noah directed his best smile toward Gaines. "I just haven't had the chance to talk to him like that in a long time."

"No problem," she lied.

Something in the kitchen started to hiss, and Noah pushed past me. Before he disappeared to tend to the food, he pointed for me to sit down. I slid in beside Gaines. I looked out the window; the neon light from the Chinese takeaway across the road cast strange shadows across the buildings, and the rumble of music came from the pub next to it. Gaines moved the bottle of wine on the floor next to her to the coffee table in front of me, watching me the whole time.

"Well, you really are being good, aren't you?" she said when I shook my head. "I'll leave it here for when you change your mind."

"What are you doing here?"

"Laura told me about your mum. I'm sorry about that."

I nodded, trying to hide my curiosity. I had a million questions about the odd friendship that existed between my sorta-wife and Gaines, but I seemed to lack the guts to ask them. I couldn't help but wonder what brought them together: top brass in the force and the leader of a local criminal gang. One thing I did know. It was more than just a book club.

Of course, I had also told Laura about Channy's visit. And now Gaines was here on her own, no sign of Bull or any of her usual guards—having hired a cleaner, for God's sake, to fix up Channy's mess. She had to be making a point?

"I understand she's not reporting it," said Gaines. "Well, that ties Laura's hands, doesn't it? I tell you, Eoin, if you find out who's responsible, let me know. I'm sure he can have an accident."

Noah came back into the room carrying a tray burdened with food and plates. There were flour tortillas, a bowl of beans, a dish of sautéed fajita-style chicken, and some grated cheese. He set the tray down on the coffee table, sat down cross-legged on the rug, and began piling his plate with food.

"What's all this for?" I asked.

"I can't cook some *scran* for my little brother and his friend? Veronica was telling me you're working for her now."

"No, no. She likes to tell crazy stories like that. I'm just a football coach, and not a very good one. The only dirty work I do is cleaning the sports hall afterward."

"You still think I'm an idiot? Look, I think it's a good thing that you've come to your senses. This is better than pretending to be a cop. *That* was not a fun phase."

"I wasn't *pretending*." That was exactly what I'd been doing. But I wasn't going to let Noah know that. "Besides, it beats pretending to be a gypsy, right?"

"Pretending? *Boshtad.* It's not my fault if you've forgotten who you are."

We both eyed Gaines in that moment, wondering how carefully she was listening. Noah smiled at me, and we both shrugged it off, the anger passing in a second.

"I saw Laura earlier," Noah said, changing the topic. "She's looking *good*, Smudge. Don't you ever think about having another try?"

"No," I lied.

"*Kushti*, mind if I have a go, then?"

He cocked his eyebrow above his dirty schoolboy smile.

"I thought you hated her."

"Well, she is a copper, true. But as far as they go, she's a good one, I suppose. Plus, you know, she looks much better without you on her arm."

Gaines laughed. The look in her dark eyes told me she was taking notes. She could order someone killed with the flick of an eyebrow. She was manipulating me in some way I was too dumb to figure. Noah finished wolfing down his first fajita wrap and then stood up and stretched theatrically.

"Well, I need to get some air. Either of you kids want anything while I'm gone? No? Suit yourselves."

He grabbed another wrap, filled it with chicken, and took it to go. Gaines watched him leave, and her eyes stayed on the front door as his footsteps sounded on the stairs outside.

"He hasn't changed," she said.

I was bothered again that they knew each other. What was I missing? I felt the urge to compete for her affection, and that scared me. I didn't want to give her any more power. She sipped at her wine and watched me for a moment.

"You really don't remember, do you? I've always wondered about that."

"Remember what?"

"Nothing." Something else in her eyes. Irritation? Had I met her when I was younger and forgotten? Had I just found a raw nerve? "I know you'll want to fix this thing with your mother. But we really do need you to deliver on Father Connolly's problem, you know that?"

"Of course, I'm not ignoring it."

"He's a sweetie. Troubled, but sweet."

"Why are you doing this? Why are you paying me to help him?"

"It's a good cause."

"Bollocks. You wouldn't know a good cause if it stole your coke money. What's your angle?"

She fixed me with those dark eyes. My guts ran screaming for the hills; my legs wished they'd been taken along for the ride. "Whatever else we may be, Eoin, our family is part of a community. My daddy and David go back a long way. You never stop being a good little Catholic boy."

"You were a boy?"

I knew it wasn't funny. She knew it wasn't funny. We let it slide.

"The church is important to the family. Always has been, always will be. This is something that needs doing, and we are in a position to provide the backing."

"I can see paying to fix a leaking roof, maybe. Or donating a new stained-glass window. Leave it to the Gaines family to find an illegal way to make a contribution."

"We're not criminals." She looked insulted. "We're a business. We make money. Sometimes we bend the laws to do it, but even we can see that some things are just wrong."

I shrugged. I'd given up trying to separate the good guys from the bad guys a long time ago. Especially since I seemed to be related to so many of the latter.

"I just don't get it. These immigrants. Why?"

"Politics and religion have nothing to do with our business. They're the first things to be forgotten when the lights go out, or when a man wants to stare at some tits. We know that better than anyone."

She leaned back into the sofa and watched me.

"I took in what you said at the club," she said. "Dragging you out there that way—I get it. You do good work for us. It's time we started treating you right."

"So you broke into my flat?"

Her smile again. "No, that was just a fun way to mess with you. But this—" She handed me a business card. "This is me treating you better."

I turned it over and looked at it. It was just a plain white card imprinted with a mobile telephone number.

"What—"

"My private mobile. No more stunts. Come work for me. For real, I mean, same as Bull. We'll cut you in. No more secrets, no more games. Gaines and Miller, just like old times."

She nodded and her mouth twitched, like she'd bitten back a comment. Then she stood to leave and told me to think about it. I could smell the wine and imagine its taste; I eyed Gaines's curves as she walked across the room to leave. I sensed temptation all around. She got as far as the front door before turning back.

"And this time, tidy up after your visitor leaves."

On the stairs I heard her talking, and then a laugh. A second later, I heard a loud and annoying knocking on the door that could only be coming from Noah. He kept it up in an unbroken rhythm until I'd crossed the living room and hallway to open the door. He was leaning against the doorframe with his wolfish smile.

"Smudge, I love that woman. I love her mind and her ass and that way she has of scaring me shitless. If you're not going to get round to making a move, would you mind if I did?"

Again with his dirty schoolboy look.

"How do you two know each other?"

He frowned, "Same way you do." He rolled his eyes in a way that said, *You're an idiot*. "When her old man would come see Dai? Or when he came to the barbecue at the pub? You remember?"

His words started to evoke a memory. A party, a celebration of something that had happened, my dad setting up a barbecue out back of the pub, my mum trying to keep me and Noah away from certain people, men who kept slipping us pocket money and winking.

"My first Wolves top," I said, the memory becoming clear.

Noah nodded. That top had come from Ransford Gaines, strong and scary, back then just Uncle Ran, who'd turned up at the party with football tops for me and Noah. That night had been the first time I wore the old gold. He brought a girl with him, a few years younger than me, and asked us to play with her while he spent an age talking to my dad.

Holy shit.

Noah smiled. "There it is. You know, for someone so clever, you've always had a knack for missing the obvious. Your old man says hello, by the way. He's staying at the camp out at Hobbs Ford. You remember where that is, right?"

"Sure."

"Go visit. Patch things up. He's not the ogre that you think he is, you know. He's just us, but older."

"I've checked the calendar, but hell isn't due to freeze over anytime soon, so I'll have to wait."

He smiled and then dipped his head to one side to cede the point. "Veronica says she'll find me work if I'm looking. Maybe it's time I settled down here again for a while."

No. No. No.

"How many times have we been through this now? Four? Five? I don't think you know what *settled* is."

He laughed, a cracked sound that seemed haunted by too many hard drinks and cigarettes. He looked around the flat for a second and then back at me. Up close I noticed a few small scars on his face, a small chip taken out of his top tooth, a white scratch down his left cheek. My big brother looked like he'd picked up a few stories out on the road.

"For real this time."

I let that one go. He'd had more second chances than I could count, but I guess that's how family works. He sat back down on the sofa and scratched behind his ear, almost like a dog. He told me that Mum had checked herself out of the hospital.

"They let her go? When I saw her she was out of it."

"Still is, but you know Mum. Stubborn. She refused to have any further X-rays, and says she doesn't want to know if she has a concussion because there's nothing they could do about it anyway."

"Has she said anything about what happened?"

His jaw tensed up. I noticed a flush of red in his face, the same anger I'd been holding back since yesterday. He shook his head.

"Has she spoken to you about money problems at all?"

"Money?" He blinked. "Nobody talks to me about money."

Money, drugs, booze. You didn't talk to Noah about these things. It was an unwritten rule, like never spit into the wind or go swimming with sharks.

"She borrowed money from some loan shark," I said. "But she's not behind on the mortgage, and she hasn't suddenly bought a widescreen telly or a new car. That money has to have gone somewhere. Once I figure it out, maybe I'll know who the hell to kill."

His face went pale, and I laughed.

"I'm joking, man. Who do you think I am? I do football coaching, that's all. I talked to Mrs. Daniels—she said she saw somebody coming round the house just before the attack."

"She say who?"

"Not exactly. She said it was a man, and that he had a *look* about him. But for Mrs. Daniels that covers everything from Bin Laden to Mel Gibson."

He waved it away. "Ignore her. She's always been insane."

"Where's Rosie? Laura said she'd called both of you."

"Yeah, she's with Mum now. Fussing over her, making cups of tea. You know how she is. She'll be preaching about something, probably."

He looked around my flat again, and this time the penny dropped. He was sizing the place up as a crash pad.

"You don't want to stay with Mum?"

He shrugged. "I don't know. It's just—it's weird, you know? I sat in our old room last night, and it doesn't feel like home anymore. It would just feel strange sleeping there. You got a spare room?"

"Yes, but no spare bed."

I watched his face fall. I pictured him the last time I'd seen him, red with rage and threatening to kill me. And now here was this new version, older and calmer. Looking for all the world like he meant it when he said he'd changed.

"Fuck it, I've got a sofa. I'm an insomniac, so you may even get the bed."

His boyish grin returned.

"Great. Now, what's for dessert?"

TWELVE

I was woken the next morning by the sounds and smells of breakfast being made. Both Noah and I had the cooking gene. We used to try and outdo each other, before we started trying to kill each other. I stretched and yawned, swinging my legs off the end of the sofa and instantly feeling the stiffness in my back. Getting old is hard to do. Noah stuck his head round the living room door.

"Hey. You better shower before I come in there and serve food. You stink, man."

"Cheers."

"And what kind of a spice collection do you call this? There's no turmeric. Your cayenne jar is empty. How am I supposed to work with this?"

I shuffled past him and climbed the stairs for a shower. Under the blast of the water my mind drifted. Connolly. Salma. Boz. Channy. Gaines. Laura. Salma again. I was pulled back into the real world by the sound of the smoke alarm, and I ran downstairs with a towel around my waist. Noah was laughing and churning his arms and legs as he fought to pull the battery out of the smoke alarm and extinguish the flames coming off of the grill.

"I might have had a little accident." He winked at me. Then he noticed the wet towel around my waist and grabbed it off me. "Perfect." He threw the towel over it the grill pan, killing the flames.

Waving away the smoke, he handed me the black and smelly towel. Then he looked me up and down.

"Cold shower, was it?"

"Fuck off."

"Hey, is that your scar? Fuckin' hell, Smudge, that looks painful."

"Yeah, it was."

It still is.

Back upstairs, I found some clean clothes and tried calling Salma. I called three times, and it went to voice mail each time. I didn't leave a message. I plugged my phone in to charge while I waited for her to call back. Noah called up to say the food was ready. He'd covered the coffee table with plates of French toast made with garlic, which was something my father had always cooked for us, and something that looked like it may have once been sausage and eggs.

"What—"

"I was experimenting. I think it went rather well." He filled his mouth with a forkful of the scrambled mess and made a face to suggest it was the best food he'd ever eaten.

"You cooking drunk again?"

He shook his head and lifted the bottle of wine Gaines had left behind. It was corked and at the same level as last night.

"I'm on the wagon."

"How long?"

"Six months."

"So you really are trying to change this time. Does Dai know about it?"

"Yeah." He beamed, and for a moment, I could see past the hard lines around his eyes and envision him as a child, grinning at whatever trouble he'd most recently gotten into. "We've got a bet running about how long I last. He keeps giving me books to read, especially stage plays by Sean O'Casey. He says it'll help."

"Does it?"

"No. I have no idea why he has me reading these things, but I'm sticking at it. And you? Mum told us you were dry, too?"

I nodded. "I am, yeah. Not for the same reason, though. Mine's health."

"Oh, mine too." His smile stayed in place.

"Yeah, different kind of health. My doctor ordered me," I said, lifting my T-shirt to let him see my scar again, "after taking out a piece of my gut."

He winced and waved for me to cover it up. Then he finished his plate of food and started on mine.

Salma called as I sat in the car outside my flat, the keys hanging from the ignition. She sounded surprised when I picked up, as though she was expecting me to live up to my shadowy reputation and be impossible to reach through normal channels. I asked her to set up a meeting with the girls who'd been victimized; she told me she'd arrange it and call back. The conversation gave me a shot of purpose, and I put the car in gear, feeling as buzzed as if I'd just downed three espressos. I slipped a CD into the player and got a blast of Ned's Atomic Dustbin as I drove. I headed into the city. I wanted to know more about David Kyng.

I got a round of applause when I walked into Posada.

The same old regulars were sitting in all the same old places. The students working the bar were different, but you get used to that in a city. Each season brought a different indie kid to Posada: each one seemed skinnier and to wear more hair gel than the last. The bar itself had been repainted, I noticed, and the old nicotine-faded walls were now glossed over with bright cream. It took me a minute to adapt.

I asked for a Coke and then did my rounds. Everyone asking after:

My health.

My scar.

My football job.

In Posada I was still treated as though my brush with fame had never happened. They never referenced the fact I'd been splashed all over the front pages of the local papers, and even appeared on the inside pages of a few nationals. They certainly never mentioned the stories that made me out to be a hero, or the ones that played up my gangland links. The only reference they'd ever made to the event was a card and CD they sent me while I was in hospital. And now, they talked to me the same as they had before it all happened.

Which was to say, they still took the piss out of me.

I settled in next to Big John. He'd been a fixture at the same table for as long as I could remember. Always with the horse racing papers and a betting slip ready to fill in. Always with half a pint of Adnams. I'd never seen him place a bet or take a sip.

"How bin ya?" he said.

"Not bad. Yourself?"

"Can't complain. Because the wife would kill me if I did." If I hadn't known him well enough to notice, I might have missed his little wink. "You aye been round for a while. Where you been hiding?"

"Wednesbury."

"Did you lose a bet?"

"Something like that, yes."

"You still working for Channy Mann?"

Everyone in town had known that I worked for the Mann brothers.

"No, Channy and me don't get on."

"That's good."

He stayed quiet after that. He returned his attention to the racing post.

"John, do you know anything about David Kyng? Works down the road?"

He shook his head. I patted him on the shoulder and stood up. My old regular spot, a small alcove in a wall with a table big enough for two people, was full. Two students were in there, sipping at bottled beer and reading textbooks. I asked the other regulars, but none of them had heard of David Kyng. I was getting set to leave, the sugar buzz from the Coke working its magic, when one of the students behind the bar called me over.

"I know the guy," he said. "He's a right bastard."

I leaned on the bar to get closer, but he waved toward the back passage. It was behind the bar area and was once the serviceman's entrance. Now it was just a cramped corridor where the regulars could have discreet cigarettes.

"So you know Kyng?"

"Well, the student union knows all about him. There's been meetings, like. Legal advice and that."

"Why?"

"He's a landlord. A lot of the students in town rent from him. He don't seem too bad as a landlord, no worse than most. But he loans money out when we get desperate, and he's a right bastard about repayments."

"Loans to students?"

"Yeah."

"I thought the university did that."

"Well, it does. But the money they give runs out, you know? And it's real difficult to get more. I could tell you stories, man. The guys who want the money to cheat? No problem. The honest ones get screwed."

"How?"

"Well, one guy in my film class? He got an emergency loan from the uni. Gave them a sob story, like, and got his doctor to sign something. He used the money to take his girlfriend to Paris.

But I've got loads of mates who actually desperately *need* the money, but they can't get it. System's fucked."

"So they go to Kyng?"

"Not just him. There are a lot of others in town these days. But yeah. They basically have to either game the system or go to Kyng. He'll give cash out to anyone because he knows he'll get it back."

"And if he doesn't? Shit kicking, right?"

"The union hasn't been able to prove anything, like. But yeah."

"Why no proof? There's a direct link, surely?"

"It's never done by Kyng, or by anyone who's known to work for him. It's always an 'accident' that happens when a student has had too much to drink on a Friday night and ends up in a fight, or whatever. The cops don't even care because it's just a scummy student, and it's bound to be his own fault, right?"

Well, the police had a point; the students in this town had always been well capable of messing themselves up. They didn't need any help.

"Have there been a lot of these *accidents*?"

"Ten, fifteen."

He sounded like a nice guy, this David Kyng.

The letter my mother had received from Kyng & Bootle had an address on Broad Street. The Gaines family owned that street. It was lined with sex shops, takeaways, tattoo parlors, and snooker clubs—and all of them tied into the family in one way or another. Did they own Kyng & Bootle?

I found the address easily enough. The entrance was to the right of a storefront loan company, the kind of place that gave poor people cash advances on their paychecks—and only asked they throw in their front teeth and firstborn as payback. The places seemed to be everywhere these days; they were this decade's version of beauty salons. The glass door for Kyng & Bootle had the company's name and hours printed on it in cursive letters.

As I pushed through I heard a soft beep, the type that rings to alert whoever is inside that company is on the way. The staircase was narrow and covered with the old-fashioned carpet tiles that could have doubled as scouring pads for washing dishes. The walls were unpainted.

At the top of the stairs was a reception area that reminded me of a dentist's waiting room. If the dentist was really low-budget, of course. The same rough carpet tile that had appeared in the stairwell covered the floor. In a bad attempt to camouflage the dirty plaster walls, there were loads of posters tacked up that offered motivational messages about climbing mountains and reaching the moon. The exact situations you need to prepare for in Wolverhampton.

There were two desks, but only one of them was in use. The man who rose from behind the desk to greet me looked to be in his late thirties and was flushed with sweat; he looked like an over-the-hill game show host. More important, he looked familiar. I'd seen him before. He was the fat man who'd shaken Marshall's hand at the Community rally.

"Hi there," he said as he reached his hand toward me. I stared at him for a moment. I hate shaking hands with a sweaty man. It's the kind of thing that gets into you and doesn't let go. You feel it all day. I reached out my hand knowing that I'd be imagining his sweaty paw touching mine the next time I ate a sandwich.

"Hi."

"I'm Davie Kyng. What can I do for you?"

He pointed to the empty chair on my side of the desk. I followed his cue and sat down. He really didn't look at all threatening. When he spoke, it was with something like a Scouse accent, but mixed up like he'd moved around a lot. His jowls seemed to move independently of his head. "I've seen you before, haven't I? Where—hang on a minute, you were at the rally last night, yeah?"

"That's right." I gestured to the empty desk. "Where's Mr. Bootle?"

He smiled.

"Doesn't exist. Bootle is where I'm from, my hometown. I just added it to the name to sound better."

"So this is a one-man operation?"

"There are a couple of people who work for me, but there's nothing like being your own boss. Nobody to answer to but yourself."

"I can imagine."

"I didn't catch your name, Mr.—?"

My mother and I have the same surname. I thought it over. *Fuck it.*

"Miller. Eoin Miller."

Something flashed in his eyes. That flicker usually showed up when a person had heard my name before.

"You're the gypsy works for Miss Gaines."

I didn't know which annoyed me more, the weight he put into the word *gypsy* or the leer he put into *Miss*. I just nodded again. Let him worry about why I was there for a moment and see what conclusions he would jump to.

"I'm paid up to date," he said. "So this isn't a business call, I take it?"

I thought I'd start subtle. "My mother's in the hospital." He blinked. Then he blinked again. "She owes you money." *Fuck subtlety.* "She's missed a couple of payments, and now she's in the hospital."

There was something in the way he seemed to be searching for a response that troubled me.

"Nothing serious, I hope?" He leaned forward and put on his best concerned face. He'd have made a good politician if he wasn't a greasy repugnant toad.

"She was attacked. In her own home." I leaned back and pulled out the letter I'd been carrying around, turning it so that he could see it was one of his. "And this little note says you were sending someone to visit her."

His mouth opened and closed a couple of times. He was clearly used to this sort of act because he started right in with the denials and the fake sincerity. "Visit, yes. If your mother's in debt with me, she'll get a few of those. I have a lawyer who sends out legal demands and some guys who follow up to discuss repayment if we don't hear back."

"And if she can't repay?"

"What are you implying, Mr. Miller?"

"I'm not *implying* anything. I want to know why you had someone attack my mother."

He sat and stared at me wide-eyed for a moment before breaking into a nervous smile, as if wondering whether I was joking. I looked at him so coldly that his expression collapsed into a tactful frown.

"Mr. Miller, I promise you that's not what I do."

I climbed to my feet, and he followed suit. He stuck out a hand for me to shake, which was just about the most ridiculous thing I could think of at that point. I ignored his gesture and gave him my best Clint Eastwood stare.

"When I find the proof—" I stopped myself short of making a threat. I didn't want to give him anything to use against me. Besides, it was time for me to get the hell out of there. I needed proof that Kyng had been involved in the attack on my mother. Also, there was the link between Kyng & Marshall. What did it mean? What was the connection?

This was getting interesting.

THIRTEEN

Salma pulled up outside my flat in her shiny black BMW, which didn't look like her sort of car. She got out and dismissed my admiring look with a wave of her hand.

"It's my brother's."

She wore tight jeans and a Sonic Youth T-shirt underneath a short red leather jacket. Her lips were very shiny, but the rest of her face was hidden by the biggest sunglasses I'd ever seen. I said that she had good taste in music, and she frowned before laughing it off.

"What? Oh, no. I liked the look of it. There was a Ramones one in the shop, but everyone has one of those, innit?"

"Can I, uh, get you a coffee or anything before we go?" I gestured behind me toward my flat. "I mean, we've got a little time to kill."

She smiled politely and shrugged a yes. I led her up the stairs and opened the front door, stepping aside for her to walk in ahead. The flat looked as tidy as I'd ever seen it, with no sign of Noah.

"Make yourself at home. I'll put the kettle on. How do you take it?"

"Black, please."

"Nice and easy, I like that."

Jesus, how bad did that sound? I ducked into the kitchen to shout at myself. *Stop behaving like an idiot schoolboy.* I made two black coffees and carried them into the living room.

"You working today?"

She took the coffee and set it down on the table. "Yes. I was recording an interview this morning for the local news. Now that it's done, I've got to go prep for my radio show."

"Oh, you're on tonight?"

She gave me a look that for a second almost resembled a snarl—it irritated her that I didn't know her show schedule. For some reason I was acting as if there weren't enough women in my life who hated me, but I cautioned myself to be nicer: I didn't really need another. A moment later, her polite smile was back in place. "It's an evening thing. It usually gets disrupted by football, but tonight is all clear."

"What will you be talking about?"

"Well, that'll be set out when I meet with the producer later. But I've got a few pretaped things to put in—you know, interviews I've already done and that. I'm trying to get someone from the police to come on and talk about dogfighting, but they're avoiding me."

Aha. This was a problem I could solve.

"My wife's on the force. I can give her a call for you."

"I didn't realize that you're married."

Shit.

Shit.

Shit.

"We're separated, really. You know how it is. Or you don't, you know...I didn't mean to imply—"

She laughed and gave me a gentle look, humoring me.

"It's okay. I *do* know how that goes. That BMW? I said it was my brother's, but it was my ex-husband's. One of the many things I got in the divorce."

"Divorce? Wow, that's pretty—" I realized too late what I was about to say, and I knew she'd realized it too.

"Enlightened?"

"I guess I should just stop talking, eh?"

Had I really just been clumsy enough to act surprised that a Muslim woman had acted in her own best interest? I looked down at my coffee and contemplated its steaming depth in silence. Salma almost managed to hide her smirk behind her cup. After she felt I'd had long enough, she put me out of my misery. "Eoin, no matter what happens, I'm not going to be sleeping with you."

I figured there was no point following up with an invite to the Ned's gig. When she told me where the first victim lived, I suggested we go in my car. We were going to a neighborhood where shiny black BMWs were not a common sight. Buried away on the Friar Park housing estate, Bassett Road had a reputation that preceded it. Council houses and anger. Front yards strewn with car parts and caravans. There were CCTV cameras mounted on the streetlights overlooking the entrance to the estate. It was a shining example of modern Britain.

I parked a few houses down from where we were going. Our arrival immediately attracted attention. School had finished for the day, and all the children walking home stopped to stare at us. Some of them moved on after a moment, but a small group leaned against the wall next to the car and cracked jokes as they waited.

Salma put a hand out to stop me as I pulled the keys out of the ignition.

"I'll start us off, okay?"

"Sure. Don't want to scare her off." I pointed to the clock on the dashboard. "Her parents around?"

"They're at work. Ruth will have only just gotten back from school. It'll be just the three of us."

As I locked the car, one of the kids on the wall offered to watch over it for me. I told him it didn't need watching; I hoped he was old enough to read between the lines.

Ruth met us at the front door with a shy smile. She was thin, too thin; I imagined that she'd inherited her thick, dark hair and sallow complexion from her parents. Her coloring was nearly identical to mine, and for a second, her eyes looked me up and down as she tried to gauge whether or not I was Polish. Her features were still too young to have character or definition, with cheeks that hadn't yet lost their roundness. Her eyes, though, were dark and attractive and showed real intelligence. She had a fresh quality to her, something I hadn't seen for a while mixing with criminals, strippers, and liars.

The house was silent and cold, sparsely decorated with pictures of her parents' family and their homeland. Even though we had the whole place to ourselves, Ruth led us up into her bedroom and shut the door. The room was small but not cramped. The bed took up most of the far wall, and a cupboard filled the space next to the door. To our right was a window overlooking the backyard, and below it was a chest of drawers piled high with makeup, magazines, and a mirror. There was a film poster for *Ghost World* above her bed, and pictures of the Gaslight Anthem competed for wall space with Tulisa.

The girl immediately went to her bed and sat down in front of her open laptop, almost as if we weren't in the room. Salma sat down next to her and tried to start a conversation. The girl wasn't ignoring us, but her focus stayed on the screen.

"Ruth, this is Eoin. He's going to help."

Ruth just nodded and watched the screen. I was dying to see what was so engrossing, but I wasn't going to step any closer until she'd accepted me.

"He Polish?"

"No, he's a Gypsy. You know, like on *Buffy*?"

That seemed to me like a reference that showed Salma's age more than Ruth's, and I figured it would sail over the teenager's head. I figured wrong. Her eyes flickered back to me for a second; she asked if I knew any fun spells.

"I'm not magic, unfortunately. I just know dirty jokes. I could probably sell you some lucky heather, though, if you wanted."

She refocused on her screen, and my eyes met Salma's as we both fell silent. I scratched my nose for something to do, and I noticed Ruth watching me out of the corner of her eye. This wasn't working. I looked at the film poster again.

"You read the comic?"

"Yes."

Almost.

"I haven't gotten round to it. My little sister loves it. *Persepolis*, too. She's always trying to get me to read that."

She turned to look me up and down again, and this time her face opened up. Just by an inch, but enough for me to notice.

"I didn't really like the film they made from that book. It's a cartoon. Did you see it? I like real actors."

She didn't have much of an accent left. Poland had joined the EU in 2004, and I guessed that Britain was all she would remember. She probably acted British at school with her friends and Polish at home with her parents. Maybe she was as mixed up as I'd been as a teenager. Not that I'd really gotten over it. I stepped in close enough to see what she was watching on the screen. I didn't recognize it, but it was clearly something involving vampires and sex. She didn't seem to lose track of what was happening even though the sound was muted.

"Yeah, I've never been one for cartoons either. I need to be able to see someone acting, even if they're really bad at it. I lose interest if a movie is animated. Unless it's *Toy Story*, of course. I could watch that shit all day."

Salma frowned at me, but Ruth got there first and said that she was a big girl who could handle the word "shit."

I tried not to laugh. Salma's shoulders sagged a little bit, and I knelt down beside the bed. Ruth smiled at me, and it changed her face. The baby fat and awkwardness of youth stretched into something brighter and more confident.

"My parents are always like that, too. It's only recently they stopped spelling out swear words when I'm around. And neither of them can spell the English words properly anyway. They're better at spelling curses in Polish."

"I tell you what, I'll swear in front of you if you promise to swear in front of me, yeah?"

She nodded. "And then you'll kill the fucker who raped me?"

FOURTEEN

Salma looked more shocked than me, her mouth open wide enough to swallow her sunglasses.

"You okay to talk about it?"

Ruth shrugged a no but answered anyway. "Sure. I don't really have anything to tell you, though."

"Did you get a look at him?"

She gave me a look that told me I'd just asked the dumbest question in the world. "He was on top of me—of course I got a look at him. But not his face, if that's what you mean. He wore a mask."

"What kind of mask?"

"Like one of those things—uh, a ski mask?"

"Okay, was it like a wool thing? Holes for his eyes and mouth?"

She shivered and closed her eyes. Wherever she went, it wasn't a happy place. She winced as she continued. "Yeah, one of those. What I remember the most is his breath. You'd think it would be the, uh, well, the other, uh, anyway, but no, it's his breath. It was hot and really bad, and it—" She shook her head.

Salma squeezed Ruth's hand and smiled an encouragement.

"It was all in my face, you know? If I opened my mouth to shout or cry, all I could feel and smell was his breath. I just wanted to get away from it."

"Did you shout?"

"Yes. Nobody came."

"Did he talk to you? Threaten you? Anything like that?"

She nodded, but it was barely noticeable. "He had a knife. He pushed it"—she rubbed her throat with her thumb—"here. He didn't need to say much after that. He just pressed it harder when I moved. For a while, I thought he'd broken through to a vein because I went numb, like I thought I was dying." Every last drop of color drained from her face as she recounted the memory.

"Okay. It's all right, just take it easy. I tell you what: let's just go back to the beginning, okay? You can skip over things if it gets to be too much."

Salma watched me with a new interest. Ruth nodded.

"We'd been at the pub, a few of us. I was meant to go clubbing with them, but I didn't really feel like it."

"Why not?"

"Just tired, and it bores me. I don't like the clubs; crap music and all the boys look the same. And the girls, the others, they have me there as a token, you know? Look how cool they are to let a Polski girl in."

"Were there any guys there with you?"

"A couple, yes. Robin was there."

Salma leaned forward. "Our Robin?"

Ruth fidgeted a little, uncomfortable. It had to be a boy in the group whom she had some history with. "Robin? Did he go on clubbing with the others or stay behind?"

She looked straight at me as though I'd just kicked a puppy. "Robin didn't do it. I'd know if it was him. I-I mean we—"

Enough said. Change the subject.

"So you walked home? Which pub were you at?"

"The Pig and Trumpet."

Across the road from my flat.

"That's a long walk, isn't it?" Salma cut in. "Isn't there a bus or a taxi you could get?"

"Standing round the bus station all dressed up at night? That would be asking for it. And the buses are worse, filled with idiots and drunks. The drivers don't do anything to help."

I asked her if she walked alone.

"Yeah. I've done it before, so I was okay. I just play my music and walk fast, let everything else go away."

"What way do you walk? I mean do you stick to the main roads or cut across fields? How do you do it?"

Salma tried to ease things along. "I know I used to cut across this housing estate. My dad would have killed me if he'd known. He said it was full of racists. One time, a car pulled up beside me and I almost screamed, but it was just an old lady asking if I was lost."

Ruth smiled a little. "In town I stay on the main roads. There are cameras and cars and all that. But after that it doesn't make sense. I mean, if I stick to the main roads all the way home, it'll take, like, an hour, right?"

"So you take a few shortcuts."

"Uh-huh. I mean, it's safer to be home quicker, right?" I nodded, and she continued. "I walked down Hydes Road. You know that way? I usually turn off at the top. There's that alleyway that leads to Oxford Street. I like to go that way and then cross the river at the footbridge. That's right by us here, you know?"

"I know the way you mean. St. Luke's Road, that alleyway. Down some steps and onto Oxford Street, then down to the riverbank. That estate's usually quite safe at night."

"Yeah. I always go that way. It's the quickest. But that night I got scared."

"What happened?"

"I don't know. It felt wrong. The alleyway gets dark. It always does. But this time it just felt like, I couldn't see into the shadows, but something stopped me. I froze, yeah?"

"Did you see anything? Hear anyone?"

"It was just a feeling, like I knew not to go down that way. You know in horror films? I felt like that. I thought maybe I'd call my dad and get a lift, but I told myself I was being stupid. So I just played a happy song on my iPod and turned to go the other way. After a while it started to feel funny, you know?"

"Funny?"

"Like I was doing all these silly things—I was talking to myself in my head and counting how many steps until I was through the shadows and all of that—and it was all silly. I started to giggle, but not too loud."

"Did you turn to look behind you at any point?"

"No, I don't know why, but it was like, like if I didn't look then there was nobody there, yeah?"

"We've all done that, yes."

"So I walked down Hydes Road. You can turn off by the school and walk along the river—you know it? Then you get to the same bridge. I walked that way, and when I felt safer again I laughed."

There was something there that was spooking her. I pushed.

"What happened when you laughed, Ruth?"

"Someone behind me laughed, too, like a mean version of mine. Kind of teasing, but worse. Yeah, like that. I could see the footbridge, and I just ran. I dropped my iPod somewhere and just ran. But then he grabbed me, and he had a knife and—"

Her mouth stayed open, moving as though she was forming words, but just a strangled noise came out, and tears started running down her cheeks. Salma pulled her into an embrace, and Ruth buried her head in her shoulder. I stood there feeling like a spare part. We waited until she seemed to have cried it all out. Then I touched the bed beside her foot, near enough to making contact without risking the real thing, and spoke as softly as I could.

"I just need to know a few more details, that's all."

She wiped her eyes on the sleeve of her hoodie.

"Was he big? Skinny? How would you describe him?"

"He was shorter than you, maybe, just a little bit. But he was strong. His arms had muscles."

"Did he say anything to you? Did you recognize his voice?"

"He called me nasty words. He said things like *bitch*. But that was all. His voice was different from what you hear around here. There was an accent I didn't recognize."

"English? Foreign?"

"No, English, I think. Or Scottish. Different, I don't know. I let him, I just—"

"Did you see which way he went afterward?"

"He just got up, laughed at me, and walked away. He didn't hurry or anything, like he knew I wouldn't—" And then she tilted her head, her mind protecting her by going in a different direction. "I lost my iPod. My parents will kill me when I tell them."

I knelt in close and put my hand on hers. It was an awkward moment, but I felt the need to make a connection. "Ruth, I know this is horrible, but you have enough to go to the police. You know that?"

She looked at Salma for a second before she dropped her eyes and shook her head. It felt like I missed something in that look, but I didn't know what it was.

At the front door I asked Salma to go on ahead and wait by the car. She paused as though she was going to question me, but then she opened the door and walked out. I hung back, out of sight for a moment, and then walked out after her. As I pulled the front door shut behind me, I eyed my surroundings, looking for any faces. Even the kids who'd been sitting on the wall had gone. They'd left my car untouched, so they had been old enough to get the message. I turned and looked back at Ruth's house. For the first time I noticed some markings, traces of fire damage around the edges of the front window on the ground floor. I wondered if they'd been burned out a couple times, too.

I almost got lost trying to drive off the estate, with its winding roads that all seem to lead back to the same place. It was almost by accident that I came across the river and realized that I was near the scene of the crime. I drove along Price Road until I came to the footbridge that Ruth had talked about. I pulled over and drummed my fingers on the steering wheel for a moment.

"Do me a favor." I turned to Salma. "Go on ahead. Walk across the bridge. We need to look at the other side. I'll catch up."

She stared at me for a second through the sunglasses, as if trying to figure me out, and then she shrugged and we got out. I leaned against the car and looked around at the houses on both sides of the river while she went on ahead. Then I followed on after a few moments.

The river looked tame, but it wasn't. I knew the current was strong enough to drag even an adult under its quiet surface. The only sign of the water's true nature was a brief drop about twenty yards from the bridge, where the river turned to churning white water as it smashed into an outcropping of rock. More than one child had never made it home after getting too close to that drop. On the other side of the bridge was a concrete path that led away to the next housing estate, and I could see children playing as they walked home; but that wasn't the way that Ruth had walked. I stepped off the path onto the grass and mud of the riverbank and motioned for Salma to follow, but she looked down at her expensive shoes and then shrugged at me.

I looked down at my feet for any signs of struggle as I walked, but the mud wasn't giving up any secrets. I would need to come back after dark, when I would be able to see things in the same light as Ruth and her attacker. I stepped back onto the path and wiped my feet, turning back toward the bridge and nodding to Salma that we were done.

"You were great in there, you know? I wasn't expecting that."

I nodded. I'd read that last part. "You didn't want me in on this, did you?"

She didn't answer, but she didn't need to. She walked on for a few steps, looking at her feet as though she hadn't heard me.

"Back there, with Ruth, it looked like she was looking to you for support when I mentioned the police. Is there something else here I should know about?"

"No." She was a terrible liar, but I let it go. "Okay, then, how about this Robin kid? Sounds like the next best place to look."

"We can see him now, if you like. But be nice—he's a good kid."

I let that go as well. Salma seemed surprised, as though she was bracing for an argument on the issue. Once she realized I wasn't fighting her, she asked a question.

"What was all that about? Making me go on ahead?"

"You really don't want to know."

"Come on. What were you up to?"

"I don't know why someone commits a crime like this, but I know crime in general. People do them because they *can*. They do them because they see an opportunity. So there's a good chance the guy we're after could live in one of those houses over there, maybe someone who saw a chance and took it. I wanted to see if anyone noticed you, or who would have the best view of you walking alone."

"You used me as bait?" She yanked off her sunglasses, and for a second I thought she was going to slap me. I would probably have deserved it.

FIFTEEN

It was an awkward drive to Robin's house. Salma was intent on ignoring me at the same time as giving me directions, which resulted in a lot of last-minute braking and missed turns. Finally, we pulled up outside a row of terraced houses in Vicarage Road, which runs up the spine of Church Hill and leads right up to the two churches that sit above the town. We sat in silence for a minute before I made an attempt at fixing things.

"Listen, I know what I did was—" I paused, trying to slow down so I'd choose the right words. "Thing is, you hired me to do the things you don't want to do, right?"

She eyeballed me and shook her head. "Yeah, but like you say, *you're* supposed to do the *things*. I'm not here to take risks. I'm just here to help the kids."

She got out of the car and walked toward the houses. I followed and caught up with her as we reached the door. Salma buzzed the button beside the heavy blue door, and it took a few minutes until we heard someone moving behind it. The kid who opened the door didn't look a day over seventeen and was naked except for a towel wrapped around his waist. His natural build was very slight—if he turned sideways, I might have lost sight of him—but he was making up for it with a lot of muscle definition. His head was crowned by a shock of bleach-blond hair, and I hoped the mullet he was sporting was a result of an accident rather than a stylist. Buried away beneath too many tattoos to count were his well-defined biceps, and I thought back to Ruth's description.

He was strong. His arms had muscles.

He greeted us breathlessly, grinning when he saw Salma but becoming far colder when he eyed me up. He looked at me with the beginnings of a challenge in his eyes. A kid's attempt at looking tough.

"Robin, this is Eoin. It's okay—he's working with me."

Robin offered me a thin smile. He still wasn't convinced, but he invited us in. The front door opened straight into the living room. Sparse and badly painted, it had a large flat-screen television and shelves full of DVDs. My cursory glance revealed Hollywood blockbusters and porn. On the wall was a poster for Newcastle United, and a few pictures of Robin and someone else. I took a closer look at the pictures. He looked like a beefed-up version of Robin. His hair was darker and his frame was wider, but the features were almost identical. He had some years on Robin, but not enough to be a parent or uncle.

"My brother," said Robin, confirming my suspicions. His voice revealed faded touches of a northeast accent. "Mike. He's at work."

Good. No interruptions.

Salma said she'd make us all some tea while he went and dressed. I heard him running up the stairs. The house was laid out like any number of other terraced houses I'd been inside before; I knew there would be two bedrooms upstairs, one at the front and one at the rear. On the ground floor was the living room, where I stood, with a kitchen just behind. Salma headed off to find clean cups and get the kettle on. I followed on and took a look round the small kitchen, which didn't look like it had any kind of spice rack.

"Does the boy know about all of this?"

"You mean the attacks? No, nobody else has been told."

"It sounds like he's close to Ruth. Would she have told him about it?"

"I don't think so, no. If it was me, this isn't really something I'd want to tell my male friends about."

As Salma poured the boiled water into the three mugs, Robin stepped into the kitchen. He was wearing combat pants and a rock T-shirt. I guessed it was rock, anyway, because it bore the name of a Japanese movie monster.

"Sorry we didn't get introduced properly before. I'm Eoin Miller. Salma's asked me to help out with the charity."

I offered my hand for a shake, and he took it in a confident grip.

"Really? Oh right, cool."

"You're from up north, I take it?"

"Yeah, Durham. My brother's a fireman, and when he transferred down a couple of years ago I came with him, like. Fresh start, you know?"

"Not quite picked up the accent yet."

He laughed and said, "I'm getting there." I asked him how he got involved with the group, and he shrugged. "Don't really remember. It just sort of happened." He looked to Salma for support, and she nodded as he talked. "I mean, I knew a couple of the girls through school, and somehow I started coming to the meetings. It was like a youth club, you know? Gave me something to do."

I nodded.

"Robin helps out, walks some of the younger children home after meetings, things like that." Salma chipped in. "He's been trying to put together a football team."

"Really? I coach a team. How close are you to a starting lineup?"

"Just missing a couple. Should be ready to go soon."

I handed him a business card for the sports center and told him we'd arrange a game. Then I changed gears before he could notice what was happening. "You walk all the girls home?"

"Not all of them. Just the ones who haven't got a ride home or live close by. Better than letting them go on their own."

"Totally. Ever have any trouble?"

"How d'you mean?"

"Well, walking these immigrants home. I mean, I've seen a fair few Union Jacks hanging from windows."

"Oh, there's idiots all right. But I'm used to them. My granddad came over from Poland after the war; my dad was first generation. We're used to the stick. But I've never had any problems walking them home."

"Is it just girls?"

He paused for a second. He was starting to notice a theme.

"No, no, guys too."

He sounded confused but not defensive. He didn't sound like he was hiding anything or trying to think of a way out of giving the wrong answer. I shared a look with Salma, and she read it right, changing the mood by asking him how his job was going.

"Great." He beamed. "I get paid to work out."

"You work at a gym?"

"Yeah, just started. Part-time, like. Cleaning up mostly, but the boss likes me to use the machines when it's quiet. He says it encourages the shy people to go on if they see somebody else having a go. Had to quit smoking, though. It was making it hell to run on the treadmill, always out of breath."

I changed up again, wanting to see if there was anything else to shake loose.

"Listen, I'll be honest. Salma's asked me to help out because some of the girls have told us they're scared. You see anything suspicious, anything at all, you give me a call, yeah?"

I watched his eyes as he said he would.

I wasn't sure whether I was seeing the truth.

SIXTEEN

I dropped Salma back at her car. She hadn't said a word to me after we'd left Robin, and she got into her shiny ex-husband-mobile and drove off without saying good-bye. I felt ready to move on as well. Making the promise to Ruth had reminded me of other obligations. And as I'd said to Salma, *no more games.*

The Apna Angel is one of the many pubs in and around Wolverhampton with a shady reputation, and yet it's one of the safer places to drink. This is because the pub is owned by Channy Mann, and he's usually holding court. If you make it past the front door, it's because he's allowing you in, and that means that nobody will mess with you while you're drinking. The pub was set back from the road, with a large car park in front. The interior was split into two sections; the left-hand side was the bar, and the right-hand side was a restaurant. And the food was amazing; the great tragedy of betraying the brothers was that I didn't get to eat there anymore.

All talk stopped as I walked in the front door. To the right I saw that the restaurant was in darkness. The pub itself was full of customers. Some were sitting at the bar, some at the tables, and a small crowd was gathered around the pool table. A couple guys even appeared to be halfway through an argument. But they all stopped to stare at me. In the dim light I could see their eyes burning into me, waiting for a false move. There was the usual Apna mix, first- and second-generation Asians with a few white faces thrown in, but there were more black faces, too. They wore gang colors, T-shirts or bandannas in red or purple. I hid my surprise. These were the colors of the Birmingham gangs. Traditionally, the reputations of Gaines and the Mann brothers had kept the gangs out of the Black Country, but Channy had lost a lot of staff and business since his brother's death, and I wondered if he was outsourcing for muscle, giving the Brummies a cut of the pie. That would change the game completely. The music was low and could only be described as *gangsta bhangra*, with a pissed-off-sounding rapper laying down rhymes over a heavy beat. I had a passing familiarity with groups like Swami and B21, but this sounded different. This was angry.

The barman was lighter skinned, with an Indian look. He had thinning hair that was cropped closely to his scalp and wire-rim glasses. His moustache matched his sparse hair.

"Help you?"

They all knew who I was. I wondered whether to bolt for the door or do the manly thing and drop to my knees and beg.

"He around?"

He stared at me for a second, just long enough to let me know who was in charge, and then he looked toward the far end of the bar and the back office. I couldn't see who he was looking at. He nodded, and after a second nodded again, this time in my direction. Letisha stepped out of the doorway and made her way down the bar. She looked to be in her midtwenties, but I knew she was younger than that. She was dressed in a shiny tracksuit, the front zipped down just far enough to show her bust, getting clear help from a push-up bra. Her dark skin was offset by simple gold jewelry.

"What you want?"

I didn't answer; I just tilted my head and smiled. I hoped it looked confident and enigmatic. She shrugged and said, "Don't move."

Yes, really. She was a comedian.

She also seemed to be taking on more responsibility than she used to. There used to be any number of lieutenants I had to go through to get to one of the Mann brothers. I used to joke about it, about how they had more people in middle management than the police. Times had changed. Letisha ducked back into the office and left me alone with the roomful of scary people watching me out of the corners of their eyes. They slowly returned to normal, the game of pool being played at a muted volume, the argument seeming to resolve itself.

"Go ahead." The barman pointed toward the restaurant door. As I pushed open the door and stepped in, trying to make out shapes in the darkness, I felt the cold bite of metal on the base of my neck. I don't care how tough you think you are; when someone puts a gun to you, it's hard work holding on to your breakfast. I smelled Letisha's strong perfume, and she pressed in close behind me.

"I'm just waiting for an excuse, fuckface," she whispered.

She pushed me forward, and I heard the door shut behind us. Something moved in front of me, and a pair of rough hands started patting me down. As the person stepped in closer, I made out his face. Marv, another one of Mann's remaining crew. After the death of Gav Mann, he'd probably become second-in-command. He should have loved me—I'd gotten him a promotion.

After he finished his search, he motioned for me to follow and walked back into the darkness. I followed, and the gun stayed pressed into my neck as I walked. They led me out back into the kitchen, sterile and gleaming white, and then down a flight of stairs into the old wine cellar. When I reached the foot of the stairs, my stomach turned over. The old brickwork and wood had been covered over with carpet, cardboard, and egg boxes, effectively soundproofing the walls and ceiling. The stone floor had been freshly mopped, but it still had a reddish tint where the water hadn't dried. The room was lit by a single lightbulb hanging from the ceiling, and the walls were lined with workbenches holding power tools. In the middle of the room were two hard wooden chairs that faced each other. Channy Mann sat in one, and I was pushed down into the other.

He leaned forward and beamed at me with his gap-toothed grin.

"Eoin, my man, how are you?"

He took my hand in his and squeezed.

"Quite a little concentration camp you have down here. I like what you've done with the place."

"This? Nah. This was Gav's room. He liked to come down here and *think*. He liked playing with tools when he was stressed. Do you get like that? I always preferred a little whiskey and a cigar, maybe a blowjob. But Gaurav? He liked to tinker and take things apart. Sometimes he'd break them."

What did I say? What could I say?

"I see," I managed to get out.

He smiled. "Yes, I think you do. You know the first time I saw my brother? He was this strange little fleshy thing wrapped in a blanket. I told my parents I'd always be his big brother. The last time I saw him? He was broken, had bits missing. He was wrapped in plastic, and the cops were asking me to identify him. Gaines's people must have worked on him until he gave up our business contacts; then they must have hurt him some more. This is the woman you're choosing to work with, eh? She doesn't even do her own dirty work."

I didn't like coming face-to-face with what had happened to Gav Mann because it was my fault. I could have reminded Channy that his brother had been doing exactly the same thing to a rival drug dealer—but now didn't seem like the right time.

"We built all of this. We worked, every single fucking day. A market stall, a van, a corner shop. We worked up to this. It's us that got our hands bloody in Smethwick every fucking night, keeping the Meatpackers in Handsworth. Veronica Gaines? She's had everything handed to her. Those Irish fucks are on the way out; they'd be nothing without their old man. You see this one?" He picked up what I took to be a router, something clearly meant to be used on wood instead of the human body. "This one is for Veronica. See, it has a lot of different settings. Here's an even bigger one," he said, picking up another heavy tool. "This one I'm saving for when she gives up her old man."

The gun at the base of my neck eased off, and I sensed Letisha had stepped back. Channy looked up at her and tipped his head, and then I heard both her and Marv make their way back up the stairs and shut the door after them. I wondered if they knew their boss had gone insane.

"Right after it happened, you know, I was going to bring you down here. Marv and Letisha, they talked me out of it. They said you were going to die in the hospital."

In my head, I responded with a number of tough-guy quips. In reality I kept my mouth shut.

"But you know, time goes by, eh? And I know you're part of the family, really. One of us." He sat back down in the chair and patted my shoulder. "So, what can I do for you?"

"I'm here about the boy."

He shook his head and shrugged. "Don't know what you're on about."

"Boz. Bauser's kid brother. He's been working for you."

"Oh, yeah, I know the boy. Angry like his brother. Bauser, now there was a good kid. They don't make them like that now, you know. This new generation? Pfft. No work ethic."

He spoke like Bauser was a long-lost veteran instead of a messed-up kid who'd died five months ago.

"I want you to leave Boz alone, leave him out."

He fingered the handle of his power tool and pulled its trigger so the tip twirled with a menacing buzz. "Leave him alone? Please. If he wants to be involved, there's not much I can do other than put him to work."

"Freeze him out. Send him back to his family. He can be better than us if he gets a chance."

He laughed. It was loud and full, and I wondered how effective the soundproofing was. "Better than me? Gyp, I'm rich. I own restaurants and fancy cars. I want something done? I can pick up the phone and call the mayor personally. *Better* than me? Shit, that boy *dreams* of being me."

I lost my sense of fear and leaned forward, face-to-face with him.

"This? This life? Drugs, guns, even that market stall you're so nostalgic for. That's what you think he wants? He just wants his family back together, and you're making him think this is the best thing in the world. You're using him, like you used your brother."

He moved as fast as he had in my flat, and something hard crashed into my temple. I felt the white heat of shock followed by something warm trickling down into my eye. I reached up and felt blood pooling around the tip of my eyebrow. He wiped down the power tool and set it on one of the workbenches.

"Here you choose to insult me?" He spoke in a low mumble that was more frightening than any shout. He slipped something small into his hand that glinted metallic, and for a second, I thought it was brass knuckles. But then he grabbed my hand, and I felt something sharp enclosing my little finger. He was holding the tip of it between the business end of a pair of pliers. "After I show you all this, after I explain what I will do to Gaines, you still talk shit about me?"

I turned to meet his eyes. I couldn't work out if what I saw in there was insanity or grief.

"I'm here for the boy. It's not about us."

He squeezed on the pliers, and they sliced into my skin, sending bright red blood dripping down my finger. I winced but held his gaze. He eased off and smiled, giving me my hand back. I wiped the blood on my jeans. I was going to need a plaster.

"I respect that, you know? I like the way you stand up for those kids. It took you a long time, Gyp, but you're starting to understand family. You still don't get the game, though, do you?"

"What do you mean?"

"It doesn't stop just because I tell him to go away. If the kid wants to work, he'll find work. A no from me means he'll just run over to Brum and find someone to say yes."

"He's a good kid."

"Who isn't?" He shook his head. "You need to decide which side you're on, and you need to do it now. I tell you what, I'll throw the kid into the deal."

"What deal?"

"The deal where I let you live. The deal where you give me what I want, whom I want. You do that, and I'll send him running to his mum with a care package. You bring me Veronica Gaines, I let Boz go."

SEVENTEEN

It's a strange thing visiting your family. You might have grown up in the house and have a key, but you still feel like a visitor. I stood at my mother's front door and rang the bell.

Laura answered.

Great.

My mother's idea of "family" was clearly different from my own. Mine didn't include my ex-wife. Sorta-wife. Whatever she was. She looked great, dressed in a halter top and jeans. Her hair had streaks in it that hadn't been there in the hospital, a mix of blond and light brown. She cleaned up well, that woman. She stepped out onto the path with me and pulled the door almost shut behind her.

"Are you okay with this?" she asked. "It was Erica's idea."

"No problem. Let's go."

We stepped inside, and I shut the door behind us. I could hear Noah's loud voice coming from the living room, holding court midway through some joke that he found too funny to tell.

I stepped into the room and got forced against the wall as my sister ran at me for a hug. Rosie was five years younger than me and, I'd always guessed, the result of the very last time that my parents had had sex. They say the third time is a charm, and that's how it was with Rosie. She was bright, funny, and far more ambitious and put together than Noah or me. She'd worked her way through a law degree and somehow made a living from moving around the country, finding things to campaign for.

"Smudge, you're late." She buried her face in my shoulder as she hugged me. She always had a way of making me feel wanted. She was shorter than Noah and me and looked more like our mother.

"Sorry. You know me, things to do."

"Yeah, right, probably some wall that needed staring down."

She pulled back and finally let me breathe, which was good because my mother followed in almost straightaway. She was still sore from the attack, which was an unexpected mercy since it meant her grip wasn't as tight as usual. She'd covered up the worst of the bruising with makeup, and she was dressed in long sleeves and a loose flowing skirt, which helped to disguise her limp.

"How you feeling, Mai?"

She smiled and shrugged. "Me? Fine."

Behind her I saw Noah manage to keep a flash of anger in check. Laura stepped into the room behind me, and Noah came up and slapped me on the back. Then he tried to regain his role as the center of attention and started telling his joke all over again. You didn't want to stand too close to Noah when he was in full performance mode. He was a very physical talker, and he would make his points with wild arms waves that could end up becoming a surprise blow if you weren't steering clear of his stage. He got that from our father, I suppose. Not from Mum—she's much calmer, always seems composed. Rosie, always the truth teller, put up a hand to stop him and told Noah the joke had fallen flat three times already.

"No, no, come on. I haven't told it yet, so shut up. Laura wants to hear it. Don't you, Laura?" Laura played along and nodded.

"There you go, Laura wants to hear it. So, anyway, there's this guy and he's working in the pub."

"Which pub?"

"What? Shut up, Smudge, it doesn't matter which pub. It's just a joke."

"You gotta set the scene, man."

"Right, okay, so it's like the Golden Lion or—what was that one that we used to live in?"

"You don't remember?"

"It was a long time ago, come on. So it's called the Golden Lion, and this guy's working there. He's working behind the bar—"

"So can we just split the difference and call him the barman?"

The women stood and watched us go back and forth trying to shoot each other down. Waiting for the edge to creep in, the point when it would turn nasty. A buzzer went off in the kitchen, and Mum stepped forward.

"Oh, that's the dinner. You boys carry on without me."

Laura volunteered to help and followed her into the kitchen. Rosie turned to me. "Are you and Laura going to patch things up?" she asked in a hushed voice.

"No, that's over. I don't know what we are these days, but we're not a couple."

"Shame," she said with real emotion in her voice. "Ah well. Mind if I have a go, then?"

Noah laughed. Then he gave her a gentle shove. "*Lakki mandi.*"

"Speak English, Noah. You know I don't understand you." Rosie pulled a face. "Besides, I get the impression I'll have more luck than you."

I asked what she meant, but she just shrugged. And then it was the three of us trying to shoot each other down. The same old tired game, going round and round until somebody won. But nobody ever won, and I had no patience for it anymore. I went to set the table as a distraction. Rosie joined me, and we pulled out all the cutlery and glasses; Mum clearly wanted to pull out all the stops to make this a proper family occasion. I pulled the table out into the middle of the room, and Rosie began setting it. I could feel her watching me. She was the opposite of Noah; she was contemplative and fixed you with a calm gaze when she spoke. She didn't move around wildly when she talked; in fact, before she ever said a word, she watched you as if taking your measure.

"How you doing, Smudge?"

"Me? I'm fine."

She pushed her tongue out at me to show her skepticism.

"Bollocks. You've never been fine. We worry about you, you know? Laura does too."

"Laura's got her own problems to worry about." I shouldn't have said that. I pushed on quickly to forget it. "It's Noah that people should be worried about. What's this sudden need to come home and settle? You believe in this new leaf of his?"

"I don't know. We've heard it all before. We'll see, I guess. Thing is, though, at least Noah's always known who he is. You? You've never had that. You jump from one foot to the other, always."

We worked in silence for a minute, the only noise the clinking of cutlery on the table. I hated these talks. Rosie had brains to spare, but sometimes she thought that meant she could talk down to her own family.

"How about you? Last I heard you were living in Glasgow?"

"Uh-huh, yeah. I was up there helping them set up UNICEF and then doing some work for a homeless charity."

"And now?"

"Good question. I've a friend down in London who wants to try suing the government for human rights violations. It's a nonstarter—I mean, it'll get thrown out at the first hurdle—but it might get some publicity. And that would be a win, you know?"

Publicity. "There's always got to be a camera, eh? No point saving the world if you can't get some press while you do it."

"What's that supposed to mean?"

"Nothing, sorry." I half smiled to show her that I regretted my snarky comment. "I got stabbed, you know. Seen my scar lately?" I lifted up my T-shirt to show her. She waved it away, and we forgot the argument. Or shelved it for another time.

The meal was large. Like a grieving widow tidying her house, our mother had buried her pain by cooking. And cooking. And cooking. Noah was subdued during the meal, and most of the conversation was directed at Laura, both Rosie and Mum wanting to know everything that had happened since her promotion. Laura had to leave out a few details. There were two bottles of wine on the table, and the women steadily made their way through them. Rosie clearly had a lot of our father in her; she buried glass after glass without showing any ill effects. Laura stopped when she knew she'd had enough, showing that kind of professional discipline that I'd never possessed.

Halfway through dessert, a homemade sticky toffee pudding, Mum began to fade and left to lie down. The food and company was making my spliced guts hurt, and I needed to take a painkiller. I didn't want to take one in front of anybody, so I stood up and started to excuse myself.

"You going to do the washing?" Rosie passed me her plate.

"Yeah, Smudge. Well volunteered." Noah grinned. It lasted until Rosie told him he needed to help. She nodded toward Laura and said they'd be fine on their own. Noah protested, looking from Rosie to me before giving up and following my lead.

Later, the four of us settled in the living room for coffee. Laura was about ready to go—I could still sense when she'd had enough. Being around my family was hard work. I nodded at her in a way I would have done if we were at a party together, letting her know it was okay to leave, but she shook her head.

A few more minutes.

Noah still wanted revenge on me for ruining his chance to tell the joke. It had been building through dinner. "You still listening to that miserable music, Smudge?"

"None of it's miserable."

"Yes, it is." Laura snorted through a mouthful of coffee. "Always some song about pain and heartbreak. I wouldn't mind if any of them could actually *sing*."

"They can sing. At least they're using their own voices— which makes it sound better and more honest. I'd rather listen to someone who can write their own lyrics and blow a note with emotion than some puppet whose voice has been Auto-Tuned to perfection."

Noah shook his head and pulled a face, waving away my defense.

"Come on, they're all fucking miserable. I caught Springsteen on the radio the other day, that Philadelphia song. Man, I was ready to slash my wrists. How've you not done yourself in?"

"They're not all like that. I mean, I actually find 'Streets of Philadelphia' a hopeful song—redemption and rest, you know? But he's written tons of upbeat songs that you'd like."

"Like what? Name *one*."

"'Born to Run.'"

"But see, that's exactly it. What's he running *from*?"

"Zombies." Rosie killed the conversation, and we all laughed.

EIGHTEEN

Laura called a taxi and then hugged each of us. She whispered it had been good to see me again, and I remembered a time when that would have made my chest fold in on itself. Now all I noticed was how the absence of that feeling hurt. Do we ever stop grieving for our past?

As though to build that wall back up between us, I slipped in some shoptalk. "We'll need to talk soon. About Gaines and Mann, I mean."

A shadow crossed over her face before she turned toward the waiting taxi. After she'd gone, Rosie, Noah, and I sat in silence for too long. It had to be the longest we'd ever been together without an argument, and everybody was too scared to speak. Rosie announced she was going to bed, probably to try and beat the odds.

"Good seeing you both."

"Yeah."

And that was it, the evening put to bed. We beat a path to the front door, and I pulled it shut behind me. The evening air had just enough of a chill that it felt crisp and fresh to breathe it in.

Noah turned to me. "She talk down to you?"

"Hell yes. You too, huh?"

He nodded. We walked out to my car, but I hesitated before putting the key in the lock. The night felt good, and it was only half an hour's walk to my flat. I tossed the car keys to Noah.

"Meet you back at the flat, okay? I fancy a walk."

He shrugged and let himself into my car. The tires squealed as he floored it. It was a small-town evening—peaceful except for the occasional passing car, and siren in the distance. A drunk was sleeping on the bench at the bottom of the street. The police wouldn't pass by here to move him. Nearby was the M6 motorway, the busiest stretch of road in the country. During the day it was a constant background hum, so ingrained and distant you didn't hear it. It was only at night, when the traffic had died away to a small procession of truck drivers, that you noticed it. You noticed its absence. I walked past a few pubs that had been closed for hours and an all-night takeaway. I turned onto Park Lane. It was a long main road that would take me almost all the way to the town center and my flat, where Noah was probably already claiming the bed. I walked past IKEA, the sounds of night deliveries drifting down toward me, and then on past another pub, the Myvod.

I reached the foot of Church Hill and then walked up it, pausing outside Father Connolly's church. It looked cold and uninviting in the darkness. My old wounds were complaining, so I slipped a couple more pills into my mouth, noticing the bottle was almost empty. I started to worry about whether I had a refill at the flat, but then the numbness took over, and I found myself walking down Hydes Road, the route Ruth had walked the night she was attacked.

At the alleyway where she had become scared, I stopped and looked around. There was a streetlight right above the path, but it was broken, and the shadow at this time of night was impenetrable, made even more dense by overhanging trees. I could stand in it and stay hidden from the road—an attacker could have done so, too. Maybe she'd been right to turn and walk away.

I turned and followed the route she'd taken down to the river, where she had turned off to cut along the bank to the footbridge. As I walked along the water's edge, the hairs on my neck stood up. Nearby I could hear the crackle of overhead electric cables, the sound mixing in with the gurgle of the river. At the footbridge I looked around again for a sign of a struggle. In the darkness it was harder to see than it had been earlier, but at least now I was seeing it in the right time frame. It was the same time of night as when Ruth had been attacked. I bent down a few times and touched the ground, looking for any marks.

While I was stooped I saw a woman from the nearby estate out walking her dog, probably a late-night potty walk. She was a couple hundred yards away, and I was out of range of any of the streetlights. I stayed still and invisible, but the woman was clearly nervous to be out in the dark, constantly looking around. The dog seemed to sense me, and it looked my way without barking. They came closer, and the dog sniffed the air, pulling in my direction on the lead. The woman was in too much of a hurry to take much notice, and she pulled the dog back as she walked toward the houses.

I felt a rush of adrenaline break through the numbness. I'd felt powerful as I'd watched her. It was a good feeling, and that troubled me. Was it the same thing the rapist had felt? I thought back to the moment I'd told Salma that maybe this was like all other crimes. But something told me this wasn't just a random john who'd seen an opportunity and seized it. There was something else there, but my drugged mind balked at thinking it through. I caught motion. It was on the other side of the bridge. I waited until I caught it again, and I realized it came from a car parked alongside the river, where the road ended. Someone was sitting in the driver's seat, barely moving. There was a spark of light, which illuminated a few basic features on a male face, followed by the glowing red embers of a cigarette that hovered in the darkness.

How long had he been there?

Since before I'd come along, that much was certain. He had to know I was there, surely? Had he watched the woman walking the dog? And, more important, had he done it before?

I waited him out, and halfway down the cigarette the engine turned over, and the headlights came on full force and illuminated the bridge. They didn't quite catch me, and I squatted lower to stay hidden as he did a three-point turn and pulled away in the opposite direction. I was able to catch the license plate as it passed a streetlight. My time on the force might not have given me much, but I'd learned to remember plates. I'd also learned never to trust my memory, so I typed the plate into a text and sent it to Becker.

I didn't expect a reply at that time of night, but my phone buzzed in my hand almost immediately. I read his text, a coded message we used when I asked him for information. *NGR?*

Not gang related?

I texted the same initials back to confirm I wasn't using him for Gaines business. That was where he drew the line in our friendship, and I'd always respected the boundary.

I was about to stand to walk back to town as the light from my phone blinked off, but something stopped me. I pressed a button again, lighting up the ground where I was knelt, and I saw something white: it was a set of earbuds, the kind that come free with an iPod, trampled down into the dirt. I looked around on the ground, and sure enough, there was an obvious depression where a body had been pressed down. To my right were three scratches gouged into the hard dirt, and I slipped by finger into them to confirm what I thought. Someone clawing at the ground.

My stomach turned, and I stood to breathe away the anger that had welled up. I picked up the earbuds and stuffed them into my pocket. Then I turned and walked back along the riverbank, onto the road, and then headed up into the town. As I turned into the side street leading to my flat, the hairs on my neck stood up again. I felt someone step in close behind me seconds before a great weight hit my right leg and swept it out from under me.

I hit the pavement facedown, the wind knocked from me, and turned over just in time to see a cricket bat flying down toward me.

I rolled out of the way, and a boot hooked into my stomach. I almost spilled my dinner onto the path beside me. Bursts of light danced at the edges of my vision as I rolled onto my back and looked up at the stars. Two figures loomed over me, their faces hidden in the shadow of their hoodies.

Both had cricket bats.

One of them swung at me again, and I couldn't find the strength to move. The bat smashed into my side, and the edge of my vision exploded with starbursts. The second figure lifted his bat and rested the tip of it against my mouth and pressed firmly. He didn't force the issue. He just left it pushed up against my teeth while his partner leaned in close to look at me.

As the hoodie drew nearer, I saw that his face was obscured from the nose down by a bandanna. It looked more like a tea towel, actually, but I wasn't in the mood to poke fun.

"You owe us, you Gypsy fuck." The voice was unfamiliar, muffled beneath the towel. "You're going to pay up."

The holder leaned on the bat, and I realized he was about to stove my teeth in. I let out a muffled choking sound and then found the guts to scream.

Then there was a different kind of screaming, and it sounded strong and angry. A shape leaped into my vision, and in a blur of movement my would-be dentist was knocked to the ground. I sighed in relief as I felt the pressure on my gums disappear. There was a solid sound of someone swinging a bat and connecting it with a body. The other hoodie turned to join in the fight, and I saw him take a hit in the face from the bat. I rolled into a kneeling position and started climbing to my feet. My vision had cleared enough to make out the scene.

Noah had one of the bats. The attacker whom Noah had just hit in the face was curled on the ground and trying to stanch the flow of blood gushing from his mouth. Noah was preparing for a second strike at my dentist, who was cowering on the pavement where he'd fallen. Noah stood between them and me and hissed out threats through his teeth.

The two hoodies scrambled to their feet and ran, leaving the extra cricket bat on the path in front of us. Noah turned and pulled me the rest of the way to my feet.

"I leave you alone for an hour and you get yourself into this?"

"Yes, that's exactly what I did. I went and asked to get attacked."

"What was that about, anyway?"

I stared at the cricket bat at our feet and remembered the last time I'd seen one of those.

"Promises to keep," I said.

———

The flames lick at the windows, climbing out of the open door.

The paint makes little chipping sounds as it cracks under the heat, and we cough a little as the plastic begins to melt and pollute the air around us.

The car was expensive. There will be hell to pay.

Until five minutes ago it had been a shiny red sports car. Imitation leather upholstery and new-car smell.

Until two hours ago it had been parked in the driveway of my school headmaster, fresh from being washed.

Now it's a bonfire. The flames reach toward the sky like praying demons.

Noah had done most of the driving because I kept stalling it every time I changed gear. He'd stopped next to every woman we'd passed and tried flirting with each of them.

Now we stand panting and laughing, ready to run as soon as we hear the sirens.

He turns to me and smiles.

"Never forget," he says.

We hear the sirens. It sounds like the fire brigade is going to beat the police to the scene. We run through the side streets of the council estate.

Unstoppable.

———

NINETEEN

My body did not want to move the next morning. It took a lot of effort—and the smell of bacon coming from the kitchen—to get me up and about.

Noah had let me take the bed, and I'd stared at the ceiling until the adrenaline had run its course and I'd finally passed out. It was the pain more than anything that woke me up. My knee and my gut screamed, and my side was covered in a light burning sensation as the bruises began to take hold. I limped into the shower and took it slowly, wincing as the warm water hit my sore body. I was becoming an expert at tending to my own wounds, and I did a half-decent job of making sure there was nothing permanent. I took a few pills to start the day right and limped down the stairs. Noah handed me a bacon sandwich and a fresh coffee.

I stared down at the black liquid and opened my mouth to tell him I'd quit coffee. But then I came to my senses and sipped at it, feeling the warmth roll across my tongue and hit the back of my throat; I wondered how I'd been strong enough to deny myself this basic joy of life.

"You feeling okay?"

"I'll live, yeah. How did you know to come find me?"

"I just wondered what was happening. I mean, it's only what, twenty minutes' walk from Mum's house? You'd been gone an hour. I was going to get the car, but I heard what sounded like a fight and figured it would be you."

"Cheers."

"Let's face it, you've always had a way of pissing people off."

"Are you the pot or the kettle? I seem to remember we threatened to kill each other once."

"Twice."

"I had them right where I wanted them, by the way."

"Oh, I could see that."

"Seriously. Another couple of minutes and I would have made them crack."

He smiled and ducked back into the kitchen. My gaze settled on a flyer for the PCP that sat on the coffee table, Rick Marshall's smiling face beaming out from the front. I picked it up and looked over the checklist of campaign pledges inside.

More police on the street.

Freeze on applications for asylum.

Smaller classrooms.

I looked for a pledge to deliver the moon on a stick, but I couldn't find one. No creativity, some people. Noah came back in with a sandwich of his own and sat down opposite me.

"Where did this come from?"

"I found it outside. Those crazies were out in the town center bright and early today; saw 'em when I went out for eggs. They're passing out leaflets and giving speeches to anyone who will listen. They spotted me as a gyppo straightaway, so I asked for a leaflet just to piss them off."

I pointed to the picture of Marshall on the cover. "Is he down there?"

"Oh yes. Got a TV camera following him round and everything. You might get famous if you go and have a word with him."

I pulled on a coat, wincing as I did so, and left Noah with the breakfast dishes. Out in the town center, it was a normal Saturday. The traffic was flowing steadily, and there was loud singing coming from the pubs. Drinking starts early in the Midlands. The main shopping street was full of pedestrians.

The rally was right smack in the middle of the action, its tables anchored just below Wednesbury's historic clock tower, which dated to the previous century. I tried to imagine this site as it had been back then: a place for public markets, public floggings, and wife selling. Those were the real glory days of this town. I took a closer look at the setup. PCP had put so much work into it, and it struck me that a rally like this had to be expensive. There were several large displays showing an enlarged version of the campaign flyer, and there was a raised podium, where I guessed Rick Marshall would be speaking later.

Spotting the man himself wasn't hard; he was followed by a TV cameraman and stopping to kiss babies.

"There are laws against that, you know," I said as I pushed in next to him.

I could see his brain spinning behind his eyes, trying to place me. But he gave me a huge smile and clasped my hand straightaway. Good old friends. He patted me on the back and turned us away from the camera.

"Did you find what you were looking for the other night?"

"Maybe. Maybe. Tell me, what's your connection to David Kyng?"

He frowned and pulled me farther away from the camera, waving a couple of times at passersby to keep the illusion going.

"Mr. Kyng? He's a member of our party. He's a valued contributor."

"Really? I thought you'd worked hard to remove his kind from your party. Wasn't that what you said the other night?"

"Look, Mr. Miller, David Kyng is a trusted member of our team, and I promise you that he is in no way—"

"You might want to watch what promises you make. I mean, as a politician, you know? David Kyng loans money out to people who can't pay, and then he takes it back in broken bones. You don't have to believe me; you can just ask around."

"Are these maybe like your connections to Veronica Gaines? You don't seem to take kindly to someone asking you about that. Perhaps you can empathize?" He sensed a victory there and eased off. "Look, I don't know anything about what Kyng does outside of the party."

"Oh, I really hope not. Because if you do, I'll come looking for you, Mr. Marshall." I stepped back as I said that last line, so that the camera would pick up the look on my face. I wasn't going to be used as a clip for a happy meet and greet.

I needed to talk to Connolly. I walked away from the town center and up Church Hill. Once upon a time, the site had been a pagan hill fort, dedicated to the god Woden. The town had been built around it, which was why you could see the two churches from miles around.

Don't be fooled, though. The town had its priorities straight; there were more pubs on the hill than there were churches.

I paused at the entrance to the church, startled by the stillness. It was a calm that seemed to grab something in me. I stood in the doorway and thought about how it seemed like the best place for me—if only religion wasn't involved. I took a few steps inside and saw Connolly deep in conversation with someone. The conversation broke up before I got to them, the other party moving away before I could get a good look. Connolly looked around the church and then came straight at me.

"You seem to like it here," he said.

"I like places that understand quiet. It can take hold of you far more than noise, if that makes any sense."

"It makes a lot of sense."

I sat at a pew, same one as last time. He sat next to me. I panicked for a moment that he was going to offer to hear my confession or give me some sage advice. He started to cough, something that came from deep inside and shook his whole frame, followed by a hollow hacking sound. He waved away my concern and then breathed deeply a couple of times before changing the subject.

"Your father was religious?" he asked.

How best to explain the culture I was brought up in? I took the shortcut. "Yes."

"I thought so."

Standing in a church on my own, I usually feel respect and grace. Held in the grip of a quiet power that comes from somewhere I can't explain. Standing in a church with company, however, I always go looking for fights and arguments. Perhaps that's why we pray alone and get married in a group.

"I need the name and address of the second victim."

This caught him by surprise. He struggled for words for a moment before he shook his head.

"No, Father, stop right there. If you expect me to do this, you have to give me her name. I need to know where she lives, to look around, to see who visits."

"And I will arrange that, but I cannot give—"

"What? Did you watch *Quincy* when you were young and decide all it takes to find a criminal is a grumpy bastard with a limp? There's something you're holding out on. I mean, I get it. I get why the families won't go to the police. That's fine. But there's no reason to hold it back from me, is there?"

He left me alone for a few moments while he slipped into a side room. He came back shortly afterward and handed me a folded piece of paper. He told me his mobile number was on there, too, but the tone in his voice made it clear he wasn't asking for a call. I felt my own phone vibrate in my pocket, but I left it there.

"I met Robin, by the way. Ruth said he'd been with her the night she was attacked. But he seemed genuine when I spoke to him."

"He's a good lad. Please, Eoin, show tact in this."

"You think I don't know what I'm doing?"

He sized me up.

"I notice you came to me for the address, not Salma. I guess it's easier to bully an old man than a woman?"

If he'd been storing that up, it was worth it. Home run. Out of the park and air out of my lungs. I had no suitable answer, nothing at all that would do. If in doubt, aim low.

"I'm still curious as to why the Gaines family took an interest in all this."

He was walking away from me now. He'd had enough of the whole thing. It was what I deserved for lobbing a cheap shot at an old man.

He paused and turned back for a moment. "I asked them to, that's all."

"And I get the impression Salma's holding something back as well. What are you not telling me?"

"Nothing, nothing at all." He was already turning away again as he spoke, but that didn't disguise the fact that he was lying. He turned back to me for a second. A mean smile played on his lips. "You're just like your father."

He walked away.

I pulled out my phone, and the screen told me I'd had three missed calls, all from a landline number I didn't recognize, but I returned the call. A woman answered, and I didn't place her voice straightaway.

"Is this Mr. Miller?"

"Yeah, who is—Mrs. Boswell? Is that you? What's up?"

"Thanks for calling back. I was—God, this sounds awful. I was looking through Marcus's room. He was in a really strange mood this morning and wouldn't look me in the eye. After he went out, I had a look through his things and—"

The line crackled for a second.

"What did you find?"

"Bullets. He's out there somewhere with a gun."

TWENTY

Finding Boz was pretty simple. First I checked the spots where I knew Mann's crew would be operating. I saw Letisha; I saw Marv. And, again, I saw Birmingham gang colors. Channy was keeping interesting new company. But there was no sign of Boz. Once I'd ruled out those spots, I called Becker and gave him a brief rundown of what I wanted to do. I drove into the center of an industrial estate and parked the car. I sat in silence for a moment and tried to plan what I would say if he did have the gun on him, but the moment was shattered when I heard gunfire.

A single shot.

I jumped out of the car, not shutting the door behind me, and ran in the direction of the shot. I already knew where it was coming from because I was the fool who'd shown Boz the location in the first place. I cut through a clump of trees and skidded down a muddy slope, coming out onto the towpath along the canal. My momentum almost took me over the edge, into the water, which might have been a fate worse than death, judging from its murky color.

Boz was a few yards farther along, standing by an old graffiti-covered bridge. His gun hung at his side, and I saw a row of bottles on the opposite bank, the middle one smashed. He turned to stare at me as I walked toward him. The fact that he hadn't led with his gun as he turned meant there was still hope for him.

"What the hell are you doing, cob? Target practice? We'll have the police here in a minute." He shrugged, and I carried on. "Where did you get that? Was it your brother's?"

He didn't answer.

"Come on, Boz, talk to me."

"What's the point, man?"

I stood and waited. His tough facade cracked, and he was a kid again.

"They let me go."

"Letisha?"

"Yeah. They said they didn't want me working with them no more. Said Mr. Mann had ordered it, didn't want me cause I was trouble like my brother."

He raised his gun and fired another shot. It went wide of the target and buried itself in the grass somewhere. Gunfire was never quite what I expected. In the limited experience I'd had, it seemed to vary dramatically from gun to gun. This one was a modest sound, a loud pop with a bass rumble.

"Come on, man, seriously. The police *will* be here soon. We gotta move." I put my hand over his gun, but he pulled away. "You just want to wait here till they arrest you? What's this going to solve?"

"Solve? Like a mystery? There aye no mysteries, man. School knows I'm thick, my mum knows I'm shit, Mann knows I'm no gangster, and the guy who killed my brother? Shit, he knows I aye nothing, too."

He lifted the gun again.

"Stop it. Now." It was the most like an adult I'd ever sounded. He lowered the gun and turned back to me. "Grow up, okay? So you can't shoot somebody. So fucking what? You're a bright kid, and you know what? You've got a woman at home who needs you. She's lost her son, and now you're dead set on making her lose another one."

I almost had him, right there. His lip wobbled for a second, and he looked like a child. Then something inside him grabbed the reins, and his adult mask slipped back into place.

"The fuck do you know about us?"

"You really want to ask that? Who stood here and saw Bauser's body? Who found the guy who killed him?" I lifted up my T-shirt so that he could see the scar. "Who took all of this to get the guy locked up?"

That was playing with the truth quite a bit, but he didn't need to know that. A siren cut through the moment, followed by another. Two police cars were almost on top of us.

"Give me the gun."

"What?"

"Look, shots have been reported, and you're a black kid with ties to a local gang. You're going in either way—give me the fucking gun."

He looked confused and didn't move. Then we heard slamming car doors and footsteps approaching from behind the trees.

"Give me the gun. They'll take you in, give you a scare. Then you go home to your mum and figure out how to fix things, okay?"

He hesitated one more moment, and I was afraid the police would see him with the gun. In the instant before the uniforms burst through the trees, he handed it to me and I slipped it into the waistband of my jeans at the small of my back. Stepping through behind the two uniformed officers was Becker, and I sent up a silent prayer to friendship. The script played out predictably because it was all for show anyway. Becker gave us both a grilling. He eyed up Boz, made mention of his gang connections, and told the uniforms to take him back to the station. As Boz was led away in cuffs, Becker turned to me.

"You think this will work?"

"Man, I hope so."

"Where's the gun?"

I trusted Becker, but I still didn't want to give up the evidence. I didn't want there to be any chance that Boz's hour in the cell could be turned into a real arrest.

"It's in the canal."

Becker squinted at me and then at the water. Sometimes the best thing a friend can do is not call you on your bullshit. He nodded and turned to follow the uniforms.

Channy had let Boz go.

That meant he'd delivered on his part of the bargain. I stared at the ground, at the exact spot where I'd seen Boz's brother lying dead. It was just another obligation that hung round my neck.

TWENTY-ONE

I was never a big reader. Books were my father's thing, and he was always trying to push them onto us. I preferred comic books, and much of my knowledge of classic fiction had come from TV and movies. I remembered Goofy in the Disney version of *A Christmas Carol*, all tied up in chains and locks, bound by the mistakes he'd made.

Obligations.

Memories.

Debts.

We let them wrap around us and tie us up in knots until we lose sight of who we are and why we do the things we do.

I was standing over a modest plaque at the crematorium, a gravestone by any other name. Beneath it were the ashes of an old man I'd once failed. I'd found him wandering in the street, on my way home from work. The last day I had felt like a cop, the last time I felt I could make a difference. He'd died without a name, without family or friends at his bedside. Somehow in the modern world we still let people slip through the cracks. Welfare stumped for the cost of his cremation, but I chipped in to give him a decent spot and a marker to show that he'd lived. The plaque was inscribed with the only name I could think to give him:

Joe Hill.

One of my earliest memories was my mother singing that song to me, over and over. The words didn't mean anything to me, but I could tell they meant something to her.

Takes more than guns to kill a man.

Well, for *my* Joe Hill it took old age, Alzheimer's, pneumonia, and cancer. Life had really not wanted him around any longer. I guess I'd pinned any hopes of saving myself on being able to save him, and when he went, a piece of me went with him.

"This was never on you, you know that?"

I turned to see Becker standing behind me, staring down at the plaque. He was one of only a handful of people who knew about the grave and its importance to me. I shrugged and turned back to my thoughts. Becker waited me out.

"How did you know I'd be here?" I asked when I finally turned to face him.

"I'm a detective."

"What can I do for you?"

He looked hurt, and for the first time in a long time it occurred to me that Becker was my closest friend. Was it too hard to believe he'd turned up to look out for me?

"Boz has been released," he said, putting on a professional face and changing the subject quickly. "I wouldn't hold out hope, though. How many breaks did we cut his brother?"

"Not enough. Boz is a good kid."

Becker nodded. "He's an angry kid. I guess you understand that more than I do, right?"

I started back along the path toward the car park. My brain was whizzing off in too many directions: Kyng, my mother, Gaines, Connolly. Becker said something, but it didn't register until he touched my arm and said it again.

"The job you're working on, how's it going?"

"Which? You mean the guy who beat my mum, or—"

He winced and then tried a shrug that came out looking pathetic. "I meant the one you tried to talk to me about the other night."

"Slow going."

He stopped and pulled my elbow so that I stopped as well. "Listen, I was a bit of a twat the other night, you know? I'd like to help with it—I mean, I do *want* to help—but it's difficult."

"Yeah, I get it. There's no case there if—"

"Yeah. But get me something, anything. Look, the main case the brass is giving us right now has to do with cigarettes, so you'd be doing us all a favor if you gave us some real police work to do."

"Cigarettes?"

He shrugged. "Apparently, one in three ciggies smoked in Britain is illegally imported. And the government, well, we know they're all cozy with big business, so they're more than happy to show their loyalty and make us investigate. Yes, these are the things that filter down our way. So your, uh, the thing—well, I want to help. Here."

He held out a piece of paper but paused before handing it over. He squinted at me. "Look, I hate to ask again, but this definitely isn't a Gaines thing, is it?"

I said no again. It felt like more of a lie than the first time.

He handed me the paper. "The car you saw belongs to a man named Paul Pearce. Guy's had a couple of driving offenses, so we had a bit of detail for him. High school teacher, lives just down the road from you. Don't do anything stupid with it, okay?"

I took a glance at the paper before slipping it into my pocket: it listed the vehicle registration, a name, and an address. I nodded my thanks and turned to get into my car before he called again.

"And, hey, the thing with your mum?"

"I'm looking at some guy called Dave Kyng. He's got an office on Broad Street."

Becker smiled and scratched the back of his head. "Yeah. I know him. We're looking at him too for a lot of things. It's only a matter of time before we find something to throw at him."

"Any pointers?"

"There's nothing I could tell you that you won't find on the Internet. Just look the guy up."

TWENTY-TWO

I called Salma. If she was angry with me for disrupting her Saturday afternoon, it didn't register above the hostility she'd already shown me. I asked her to set up the meeting with the third victim, the one she was willing to introduce me to. She said yes, but there was a lot of background noise, and she had to repeat herself a couple times.

"Where are you? Sounds like there's a riot going on."

"Villa Park. Me and my brother have season tickets."

"Villa? You're a *Villa* fan?" Her support of a Birmingham team was a personal betrayal of everything I held dear.

"My dad lived in Aston before I was born, if you must know." Was that a trace of defensiveness in her voice? Excellent. Victory for me. "He used to take us to the games when we were little."

"Look, it's going to be okay. Everything will be all right. There's still time. Wolves are playing tomorrow. You can come with me to the game, and we may be able to save your soul."

She was still laughing when I hung up.

I drove to my mother's house. She hated football. Saturday afternoon was the one time of the week you could guarantee she'd be indoors, so as to avoid the drunken fans who'd be out and about, and fighting to find something on the television or radio that didn't involve sports.

Rollo came to greet me as I parked outside. It was not a friendly greeting, more of a cold stare, a reminder that he could kill me if he wanted to. He followed me up the path to the front door and ran around my feet as I rang the doorbell. As soon as the front door opened, he was a blur, vanishing into the house.

Little fucker.

It was Rosie who answered, looking tired and disheveled.

"What? Just wake up?"

"After you went last night, I changed my mind and went out. Thought I'd see what the local clubs were like these days."

"And?"

"Eh, I don't really remember, to be honest, so it was either great or awful."

"Anyone hiding back there that I should know about?"

She pulled a face and turned to climb the stairs, leaving the front door wide open for me. "Funny. You're funny. Now let me have a shower. Maybe several."

I stepped inside and shut the door behind me. I pulled off my jacket and draped it over the banister at the foot of the stairs. Then a brief flash of memory hit me.

I'm falling down the stairs. I don't know how, but I remember the carpet slipping beneath my feet at the top. Then it's all a blur. My legs crash into the wood; the corners of each step jump up and down at me as I slide down. I hit my head and see stars. The tiled floor reaches up to smack me in the face, and I decide it's easier just to lie there, staring at the tiles, noticing all the dust. There's a crashing sound in the living room, and then my father appears—or, rather, his feet do. He lifts me up, and there's panic in his eyes. I realize I'm crying, and he's dropped whatever he's doing to come and pick me up. I'm in pain, but I feel good.

I shook the memory off and walked down the hallway, pausing for a second at the living room door. I could hear my mum inside, fussing over Rollo, and I wished I could avoid the conversation I was about to start. When I pushed through, she smiled at me and started to get up out of her chair. I put my hand out so she would stay put and bent down to kiss her on the cheek.

"How you feeling?"

"Better now I've seen my boy."

I shrugged that off. I'm not good at sincerity.

"Dinner was good last night. You enjoy it?"

"It was good having the family together, even Laura. It never seems to happen anymore, does it?"

"Did it ever?"

She didn't answer right away, and I wondered if I'd upset her. Then she must have seen me looking at her bruises, and she told me not to worry. "You've got another fifty years of me yet. I'm going to live long enough to patronize old people. I'm going to be able to wink at a ninety-year-old and say, 'You'll understand when you're older,' like they always do to me now."

"Yeah, we're stuck with you—I'm not worried about that. Though does this mean I'll be too old to enjoy my inheritance?"

"You'll never be too old to enjoy the tin of coffee and packet of biscuits that I'll leave for you in the will."

I sat on the sofa opposite, and the cat brushed against my legs. I ignored him and stared at all the photographs on the wall: school uniforms and bad teeth, summer holidays, my wedding.

She followed my gaze and smiled. "You looked all grown up that day. Suit and tie. You'd even combed your hair."

"Never again."

"Laura's doing well for herself, though, isn't she? I mean she always seemed the type, but still, it's good to see a woman doing so well."

"What can I say? I'm a lucky charm."

"Get off. That girl's worked her ass off, and she's gotten a good job to show for it. She was in the newspaper again this morning, talking about a new antidrug initiative they're doing."

She passed the paper across to me. It was turned to the second page, where Laura was pictured with some schoolchildren holding a banner that proclaimed they all said no to drugs. I looked for the disclaimer that stated that she didn't say no to drug money from the Gaines family, but they had left that bit off the banner. I sat and waited for the rest of the speech: *If only you had followed her example, you'd have a good job yourself.* But it never came.

"How are you really feeling?" I said. "You in much pain?"

She shrugged. "Not really. It's not the first time I've had a kicking. Used to happen a lot when we were living in the caravans."

That had been the first stage of our family life, before she'd convinced my father to turn to the settled life. To do things her way. To get the pub, and then this house.

"Who did it?"

She ignored the question, so I asked it a second time.

"Just forget it, okay? I know I have."

Her eyes told me a different story, and I knew they told the truth. I have a little theory: once you learn that Father Christmas isn't real, your parents lose the ability to lie to you. It had been quite a long time since I'd believed a lie from my mother.

I told her that Mrs. Daniels had seen who did it, but I left out that she was too old to give a report that made any sense. Mum looked at me for a split second with something in her eyes that I couldn't place, and then her usual mask reappeared.

"Come on. Tell me what happened. I can deal with it."

"Deal with it? *Deal* with it? How, through the Gaines family? What, you'll have a word and the problem will just disappear?"

I didn't even need to ask how she knew. She always knew, somehow, when I was doing the wrong thing.

"Mum, it's not—"

"Don't—I've had enough lies from the men in this family. And I've had enough of *that* family, too."

"What exactly did Dad do for them?"

"You'd have to ask him."

"I'm asking you."

"I tried so hard." I watched the hinge of her jaw clench beneath her skin. "I knew I couldn't change your father, but I was damned if I was going to let my boys turn out the same way." She looked at me. "Noah was one thing. He'd always known too much. But you? You listened to me when I told you not to talk to the wrong people. Then you joined the force. I thought at least I'd saved one of you."

I felt my cheeks flush and burn. I felt shame. I reacted the only way I knew how—with sharp words. I pulled out the debt letter I'd taken from the house and threw it at her.

"What's the money for, Mum? If you needed something, why didn't you ask? You know I've got money in the bank—"

"I don't want dirty money. I've had enough of it."

"So you'd rather get in over your head with a loan shark? Is that how it works? Christ, Mum, I'm trying to help you. Just tell me this is the guy. Just tell me. I'll make the debt go away."

She stared at the letter but didn't say a word. The worst kind of silence settled over us, and it seemed to stretch out forever. Until she quietly folded the letter and placed it on the table beside her.

"Get out." She didn't look up as she said it, keeping her eyes fixed on some invisible object resting on her knees. "Now."

TWENTY-THREE

Salma pulled up outside my flat in her expensive car and opened the passenger door for me to climb in. She didn't say a word, just pulled away from the curb without waiting for me to shut the door. She ignored me as she accelerated. Then something in her seemed to snap, and she braked suddenly and pulled the car over to the side of the road.

"I'm not looking to play any games with you, you know?"

Games? What games?

"Like, all the funny banter, the teasing, the trying to win me over with your awkward charm. I'm not falling for any of that crap."

Oh. Those games.

I didn't want her to see she had a point, so I changed up. "Look, have I done something to offend you?"

"What do you mean?"

"Ever since we met in the church, there's been something bad between us. Like you're holding a wall up, or you don't want me around."

She shrugged. "I guess. When Connolly mentioned you, I asked around the newsroom. I didn't like what I heard."

I thought of that old joke. *You can do a hundred good deeds, but once you fuck just one goat...*

"Yeah, I thought so. But then you meet me, and I'm not Freddy Krueger, and I don't spit fire. But you feel angry at me because you can't stay angry at me."

She stared at the steering wheel for a moment. Then her shoulders relaxed. She put the car back in gear.

"You're right," she said. "You're not what I was expecting. And I've been holding that against you, I guess. I prefer it when people live up to my expectations. I don't like surprises."

"And you're a woman, and I've been holding *that* against you."

"Sexist." She laughed and shook her head, and after that the silence we drove in wasn't a tense one. She drove us to Thorn Lane, a small cul-de-sac situated in the shadow of Church Hill.

The cul-de-sac was set back from the road and ended at the brick wall that signaled the start of the next housing estate. To the left was a row of council garages, hidden from the road by houses, and a dirt path that ran behind the back garden of each house. To the right was a row of flat-topped low-rise council flats two stories high. The ground-floor flats opened straight out onto the car park, and the top-floor flats each had their own staircase and balcony. Some of the doors to the ground-floor flats were propped open, and a group of children was running around in front of the garages chasing a football.

Salma answered my question before I had time to ask it. "Asylum seekers."

"This is the land of milk and honey, huh?"

"It's the land of wherever the council can put them, yes."

"Are they expecting us?"

She nodded. "Well, they're expecting me. I'll explain your presence somehow. Our charity works with most of the people in the block, and one of the kids is having a birthday party." She reached round to the backseat and came back with a present wrapped in bright red paper. "And, listen. I know after our meeting with Ruth I don't need to say this. But be tactful, okay?"

I followed her up the steps of the nearest flat. The front door was propped open, and we could hear the sounds of children laughing and shouting inside. Salma rapped on the door and then stepped inside. I followed her through into the living room.

Dozens of children were huddled into the small room, playing with a few toys and watching an old television set. They all turned to look at us. First they saw Salma, and their eyes widened with excitement, and then they saw me and settled back down. One of the children stood up and ran at Salma, wrapping his skinny arms around her in a tight little hug. She bent and whispered something in his ear in a language I couldn't place and then handed him the present. He squealed and tore into it, revealing a plastic robot, which was clearly the best thing he'd ever seen. He held it over his head and ran back into the crowd of children. They clamored to get a closer look. Bribery had done its trick—they'd forgotten all about me.

Salma led me out into the hallway again and spoke in a low voice. "Stay here."

She opened the door to the kitchen and stepped in. Inside was a group of adults leaning on the cheaply fitted countertops and drinking bottled beer. One of the women eyed me for a second and then pushed the door shut to keep me out. She had looked familiar, short and slim, with Eastern European features and short dark hair. I knew her from somewhere but couldn't place her.

I stood in the hallway for a second and listened. In the living room, the children laughed and played. The hallway was painted in a faded cream that looked like it had been gathering grime since the seventies. I behaved for as long as I could—about two minutes—before questions at the back of my mind forced me to start exploring. I walked past the kitchen door and opened the next door I came to. It was a cramped bathroom, the countertop lined with the usual selection of soaps and razors. The sink was stained with toothpaste and soap, and the shelf above it held close to a dozen toothbrushes.

I opened the next door and stepped into a sparse bedroom. A single bed was pushed against the back wall, and the remaining floor was carpeted with wall-to-wall pillows and mattresses. Half a dozen neatly folded sleeping bags were stacked below the window. The only other item in the room was a portable gas heater.

I pulled the door shut quietly and tried the next one, but it was stiff and I knew I couldn't open it with without putting some weight behind it. I didn't want to make that kind of noise, and I already had some of the answers I'd been looking for.

I retraced my steps to the living room and leaned on the doorframe, watching the children play. I looked at the faded clothes they were wearing and listened to the various languages they seemed to be using. All pieces of a puzzle that had been eating at me. There was a new fire extinguisher next to the front door, and I noticed that smoke alarms had been fitted to the ceiling in the hallway and the living room. It seemed at odds with everything else.

The voices in the kitchen got louder, and I realized Salma was saying good-bye to the parents. She opened the door and walked toward me. I saw the adults peering at me suspiciously, and the small brunette locked eyes with me again. From her expression I knew she recognized me, too. She smiled, and I caught what I'd been looking for. I knew where I'd seen her before.

Salma stopped and peered at me. My expression must have given me away. She started to form a question, but stopped. We both knew the score.

"How many of the people in your group are illegal immigrants?"

"I, uh—"

"I knew you and Connolly were holding something back. *That's* why you can't go to the police." I was only getting warmed up. "At least one of the women in that kitchen dances at Gaines's club—I know because she's danced for me. Is that where the money is coming from?"

"That's not quite how it all works."

"*Not quite?* This is human trafficking."

She slapped me. I hadn't expected that, and it seemed like she hadn't either.

"I'm sorry," she said, looking away. "But that was a horrible thing to say. Connolly and me, we're helping these people, not trading them."

"Okay, tell me what's going on."

"It's a long—" She realized it didn't matter how long a story it was going to be. She nodded for me to follow her outside, and we sat on the low wall beside her car. "It started out fine—normal, I mean. Just like we said. That was back when there was money going around for community projects, and we could get lottery grants. But after that last election the money dried up."

"Cutbacks?"

"Yeah. That and the fact that they turned *immigration* into such a dirty word at the last election that all the private funding went up in a puff of smoke. Everybody was too scared." She took a deep breath, like a child who was all cried out. "Then this businesswoman comes in and offers help, says she can take all her donations as tax write-offs as long as we keep it local. I thought she just wanted to help the local community, you know? But eventually I figured out she had other reasons."

"Veronica Gaines."

She nodded.

"I didn't know what she was really into. She showed me her businesses, the legit ones, and they're all—they look good, you know? Positive stuff. Public sports centers, beauty salons, restaurants. But once we were taking her money, she started adding all these strings."

"How does it work?"

"I did a report on money laundering on the show a few months back, and the way it's described? We're doing a very similar thing. It's like person laundering. We have enough legitimate work to do, enough legal immigrants and asylum seekers, that we can layer in the illegal immigrants without making waves. Give them homes and jobs. You know how many companies pay people below minimum wage by doing it in cash, off the books?"

"You're happy with that?"

"No, but it's a start. When my dad came over? There was no minimum wage. He was a qualified doctor, but over here he was nothing and nobody. Took him ten years to get a decent job, and he's still trying to win back the self-respect that was stolen from him. These people are getting a start. They're getting regular wages, and support, and a community. These kids will grow up not seeing their parents treated like dirt."

"They'll see them as lap dancers and unprotected workers. You know where this leads, right? You're supplying a new working class. These people won't get paid minimum wage, and they'll never have employment rights. These flats?" I pointed to the flophouse we'd just emerged from. "They're a modern poorhouse."

"These people come from places where they don't have any rights *or* wages," she said. "Being working class is a step up for them. You want to lecture me on morality? You said yourself that one of them danced for you." She hit on the one thing I'd hoped she wouldn't, and it hurt. "Where was your anger at the way they're treated when you were getting your dick wet?"

We sat in silence for a long time. I was fighting for a balance between anger and guilt. Salma was probably fighting to stop herself slapping me a second time. We were both slowly winning our battles. Then she spoke, this time sounding quiet and tired. "We do good work. We're helping them. We're getting them into homes, and jobs, and connecting them to friends. We don't make them come over here, and if we stopped trying to help, they'd still come anyway. At least this way they have someone looking out for them when they arrive."

"Where does Gaines get them from?"

"I don't know. Really. I think there's some cartel she has a deal with. But I don't ask. I don't want to think about it more than I have to."

"And Connolly, he's in on this?"

She shot back upright at that. "No. He was the one who originally contacted Gaines about funding, so he guesses some of it, sure. But he doesn't know the worst of it. He only hears about the happy endings. Hearing the truth would kill him."

"I wouldn't want to be the person to explain to him the truth about happy endings." I tried for the joke, but it didn't connect. Then I took it down a notch. "This is the real reason you've been off with me, isn't it?"

She thought for a moment and then said, "Yes. Look, I'm not happy with all of this. It's not what I set out to do; it's not what I *want* to do. But I can't confront Gaines about it, and I can't hate myself more than I already do. You're the next best thing. God, that sounds horrible, doesn't it?"

I shrugged. "Forget about it. People usually hate me for far less rational reasons than that. But now I want to know. How high up does this thing go? I mean, I noticed the smoke alarms and the new fire extinguishers. Someone did a fire and safety check on that place. Have you guys got an insider at the council who's covering for you?"

"I don't know. That would be Gaines's end of things. I arranged the fire inspection, though. Robin's brother, the fireman? He did that, and he checked the water and electricity too. These people get better care from us and Gaines than the legal ones get from the council." She peered at me, trying to read my face.

I cut to the chase. "Which of the victims are illegal?"

"Bejna, the one you're meeting today; her mum didn't want to risk being turned down, so she came in illegally." I could see Salma working hard to keep the fear out of her eyes. "Are you going to report us?"

Illegal immigrants or the man preying on the youngest and most vulnerable of them—which did I care about more?

Fuck it.

I said, "No. Whoever is doing this, he's not just some guy on the street. He knows about all of this. It's someone you've trusted. He thinks he has a free pass because you can't report it."

Young girls can be raped if they don't exist.

An old man can die without a name.

Families can be burned out of their homes if their skin is the wrong color.

I need to live in a world where the tree makes a sound when it falls in the rain forest, even if there's nobody there to hear it. I need people to matter, things to matter, because then maybe I will matter.

TWENTY-FOUR

Salma led me to the third staircase in the complex of apartments. She motioned for me to lead, so I climbed the stairs in front of her. A woman was waiting for us at the top. She was wearing some kind of shop uniform, and her dark brown hair was swept back from her forehead; it was frayed as though it had been tied back all day and only just released. Her skin was a shade darker than mine, but that didn't help me pinpoint her ethnicity. She wasn't overly feminine, but she was well drawn and had an attractive face. The best word to describe her was handsome. She eyed me with a bemused expression.

"So this is him, yes?"

Her words were thicker in the middle, her accent carried something of Eastern Europe or the Balkans, but that was as close as I could get.

"Yes. Sally, this is Eoin. Eoin, Sally."

I shook her hand; she had a cool and firm grip. "Hiya, Sally. What's that accent? Russian?"

She snorted and looked again at Salma, keeping her eyes off mine. "Russian? How does he get Russian? Have you brought an idiot to help us, Salma, eh?"

"Sorry, I—"

"Oh, he's sorry." She turned to me now. "You hear my accent, and you call me Russian? I should laugh at you. I do, in fact. Is okay, though. If you called me Turkish, I would have spat at you."

She turned and stepped back into her flat. The hall was exactly the same as the previous one, down to the new fire extinguisher. She led us into the living room. The furniture was secondhand, and the floor had been vacuumed more recently than my own. There was a dining table beneath the window, next to the door we'd come in through, and it was piled high with school textbooks.

"Please, please." She pointed us to a space on the sofa after moving away newspapers and magazines. "You want to drink?"

Salma answered for both of us, saying I'd take a Coke and she'd have a tea. I went along with whatever she said. Every time I opened my mouth, I said the wrong thing. Sally disappeared into the kitchen to get the drinks.

"She's from Turkey." Salma talked low while we were alone. "But don't tell *her* that; it's a sore issue."

"I thought the Kurds were in Iraq."

"There too. And Iran, but—"

"We are lots of places." Sally came back in carrying our drinks, and I wondered how much she'd overheard. "They say we are largest, um, group? Largest group without a home. Not true. We know where our home is, but it's not on the map. They took Kurdistan from us. So now they call us homeless."

"I know how that works. My family are Roma."

"Let me look at you. Yes, now I can see it. Good people, *Rom*, good friends to my family when I was a child. Would come when crops were ready to harvest, work with us for food. Eh, it was a long time before now. They moved away—everyone moved away. I did too, but not for a long time."

"What made you move?"

"We are treated like shit. In my own country I am not allowed to speak my language. It is against the law. If Kurds try to talk politics, they are taken away. My brother was taken away. We didn't see him again."

"So you came over to get away from that?"

"My daughter, Bejna, I came for her. And for my husband."

"Where is he?"

The air seemed to go out of the room for a second, and from the corner of my eye I saw Salma wince. I knew what the answer was going to be before it came, but Sally seemed willing to talk about it anyway.

"They say he was enemy of Turkey. They say he was planning to start a riot and that he was danger to everyone. They came into our house at dawn and beat us. They took him, and I never see him again."

"So he started talking politics too, like your brother?"

"He was—" She looked to Salma for a second as if she had forgotten the word. "Journalist. He was a journalist. He wrote the truth. He wrote about his friends and his home, and it killed him."

Saying that last part took something from her physically. Her whole body seemed to tremble for a second after she spoke, and it looked like she folded inward.

"The day after that, some of the soldiers came back. I thought, to take me also. But they didn't come to arrest me. They said there was no man in the house now and that made me a whore, and that they would treat me as one. They took turns. After they left me alone, I got Bejna dressed in her winter clothes. I borrow money from next door, and we started walking. I brought her here to have a good life."

I dropped my eyes from her gaze and sipped my Coke. Not for the first time it felt like my job to be ashamed simply for being a man. Salma gauged exactly the right amount of silence to observe before she continued.

"Where is Bejna?"

"She is in her room. I wanted to look this man in the eye before I let him ask my daughter those questions. I have to see what kind of man he is, yes?"

I nodded, wondering what conclusions she'd come to. I couldn't blame her if she didn't like me. If anything it would show she was a good judge of character. "Sally, I know you came in illegally, but you'd have a good case to stay officially, and it's possible the police would be able to catch the man who attacked your daughter."

"The men who came into my home and hurt me, the men who stole my husband? They were police. They wore uniforms the first time they came. The second time they didn't."

Salma touched my knee and explained quietly. "I've looked into it, and they do have a case to stay. But Sally feels the law would make an example out of her and deport her before the hearing."

"Example, yes." Sally shook her head. "I have been made example before."

"What are you hoping I'll be able to do? If I find him, I mean?"

"I do not know. That's the truth. I would like that Bejna is safe."

I nodded. Whatever Sally had been looking for, she seemed to find it in that gesture. She turned and called out her daughter's name, facing in the direction of the bedroom as though that would help the sound travel through the wall. I heard movement, a bed creaking followed by a door opening. Soft footsteps padded along the hallway and paused for a moment short of the open door. Sally said something low and soothing in a language I didn't understand, and then Bejna stepped into the room.

She looked very different from her mother, but it was clear they were blood. Bejna had the same posture, the same set to her jaw. She was taller than I expected, around five ten, and striking. If Ruth's body had been mixed up, caught in the moment between being a child and an adult, Bejna was already coming out the other side. Any baby fat she might have carried was gone, except for a little softness in her face. Her skin was lighter than her mother's, and her hair had more strands of dark honey woven through the brown. She was rail thin, but it was obvious that in a few years' time she would be stunning. She had wrapped herself in a bathrobe though she was fully clothed beneath; I could see a T-shirt in the V of the robe, and jeans stuck out of the bottom.

It was when she stepped forward and walked across the room that she began to look like a little girl. Women are aware of their bodies in a way that girls aren't, and Bejna clearly wasn't ready yet for what her hormones were pushing her into. I had a moment of anger as I thought about what could be waiting for her as part of Gaines's system. Would she get a choice? She sat at her mother's feet and smiled at Salma, and then she looked shyly at me.

I knew I needed a way in, to make a connection, but there were no film posters for me to cheat with. Instead, Sally held her daughter's hand and coaxed her through it. Bejna talked to her mother for a while in a mix of English and what sounded like either Turkish or Kurdish. She was biting her thumbnail as she spoke, and occasionally she glanced at me nervously.

Eventually Bejna spoke to me. "Can you make this go away?"

TWENTY-FIVE

"Do you go drinking with any of the girls from the group?"

She shook her head. I wondered if she would tell a different story if her mother wasn't around, but I got the feeling she wouldn't answer my questions if she didn't have that hand holding hers.

"I don't like to drink," she said. "It gives me a headache, and I talk too fast. People can't understand what I'm saying. I don't like that."

Cross the pub off my list.

So far, I had two victims from different cultures, different countries, who had immigrated for different reasons. They lived in different parts of town, and they didn't drink together. I needed a connection between them. The community group was the only thing they had in common. But there were a lot of girls in the group, and only three of them, as far as we knew, had been raped. If I could find a second link, I would find the man responsible.

"Okay. We can stop at any time, yeah? When did it happen? Was it after one of your group meetings?"

"No, no. I had been to the cinema with Robin."

"Robin was with you?" Salma and I shared a look as Bejna nodded. "Which cinema did you go to?"

"The Showcase down at the motorway junction? You know it? Yeah. We go there—went there—every week after school. They have a cheap night, and the tickets are half price."

"Was there anybody else there with you?"

She shook her head. "No. Usually there would be, but that night it was just us. The others were busy."

"Who else normally goes?"

She looked at Salma rather than me as she reeled off names. The only one I recognized was Ruth.

"Was Ruth supposed to be there that night?"

"Um, no. They had fallen out, Robin and Ruth. Had an argument."

"Really? What about?"

She blushed, and the story told itself. Teenage hormones. Someone fancied someone. Someone else fancied someone else. It all went round in circles.

"Okay, how do you get to the cinema? Bus?"

"No, there isn't one that goes the right way. We walk, maybe sometimes get the bus half of the way. Sometimes people drive us."

"Walk? That's a long way, especially when it gets dark."

I looked out the window. The evening was already setting in. The children were still playing football. I could hear the ball skidding across the pavement. The walk Bejna was talking about would have been three or four miles along main roads.

"She always told me they got the bus," Sally said. "Always. I would never let my daughter walk all that way. Never."

"It wasn't the walk!" Bejna shouted before taking a breath and regaining her composure. "It wasn't the walk. It didn't happen by the cinema. It was right—" She stopped and wiped away a tear.

"Where was it, Bejna?"

She pointed in the direction of the road outside. "Over there," she said. "The other side of the road."

Right outside her home, where she should feel safe.

I walked over to the window and looked out of it. On the other side of the road was a small field, a triangle of land between a house and a warehouse. There were lots of bushes and no streetlights.

"So Robin wasn't with you by then?"

"No. He always offers to walk me all the way here, but it's out of his way, right? His house is up the hill, and I'm a big girl."

"Okay."

"I was walking down the hill, right over there. And then I got hit on the back of my head." She rubbed a spot near her crown. "Before I knew it, I was being thrown against one of the trees. I landed in the dirt. I got scratched, all here."

She pulled up the sleeve of her bathrobe to show marks on her arm. The scratches were well on the way to healing, but they would have caused a lot of pain at the time.

"Did he threaten you? Say anything to keep you from screaming?"

"He never said anything, but he had a knife." Her hand went to her throat involuntarily, resting there protectively. "He put it here, kept pressing it. When he got to the end, when he was getting excited? He was pressing it so hard I thought he'd kill me. I thought he'd cut me, but he hadn't."

Her jaw looked as if it was starting to lock up at the memories, and I knew we didn't have long before we'd need to back off and leave her alone.

"Did he hit you again or run away? Anything like that?"

"No. When he was finished he just, he just left me lying there and walked away. He walked. Like he didn't think about me after that. He just walked away and laughed a little."

"Did you recognize the laugh? Was it one you've heard before?"

"No, it was nasty. Mean."

"Was he wearing a mask?"

"Yes, like the bad guys wear on TV. A black one? Like that."

Generational thing. To people my age, a balaclava or ski mask meant IRA. To people Bejna's age, they were worn by bad guys on TV.

"Did you notice anything else about him?"

She thought for a moment, and I knew this was the last answer we were going to get. There was a distance taking over in her eyes; she was zoning out, fleeing to a place where it didn't hurt to be.

"Cigarettes. His clothes and, yeah, his breath. It was horrible."

Sally slid down off the chair to wrap her arms around her daughter, and they rocked slightly. I was losing her, but I still needed just a few more details. It still felt like there was an obvious question I was missing. I waited a few seconds, and then started again, quieter. "How did you all meet? Was it at the group?"

She shook her head and said something inaudible into the sleeve of her bathrobe, and then she realized I hadn't understood and repeated it louder. "At school."

School.

The most obvious connection among any group of teenagers, and something I'd never thought of. "Do you know Paul Pearce?"

"Mr. Pearce, yes. He does PE."

"Did he teach all of you?"

She shrugged and then sank farther into her mother's embrace. Salma and I both said quiet good-byes, and Sally nodded.

TWENTY-SIX

Salma asked me what the next step was, and I told her I wanted to check out a couple local addresses. I told her she could leave me there since my flat was within walking distance, but she shrugged and said she had no other plans. I agreed she could tag along, but I insisted that we change cars. Hers stuck out too much.

The third victim was Rakeela Mahmoud.

According to the address I'd bullied out of Connolly, she lived on Hobbs Road. If Salma was surprised that I had the address, she didn't show it as we pulled up under the shade of a tree a few doors down on the opposite side of the road.

Hobb was an old Black Country name for the devil, but this street seemed like the opposite of anything wicked. The houses were quiet and well kept, with TVs flashing in a dozen front windows. There were none of the rough edges I'd felt on Bassett Road nor the poverty that had hovered over Thorn Lane. The streetlights buzzed away, and the occasional teenager walked past, head bowed, staring at scuffed trainers.

"What are we here for?" Salma sounded genuinely interested.

"Even if I can't talk to Rakeela, I wanted to get a look at her, get a feel for the street. See if there's anything wrong."

"How would you know?"

Good question. "There's no real science to it. I just know when something's wrong. It's one of those senses we developed back when we slept in caves and defended ourselves with rocks. I've learned to trust my guts—they tell me if something is wrong."

"And what are they telling you?"

"There's nothing wrong."

She laughed. It was easy and real; whatever walls she'd put up before seemed to have gone now. I smiled back at her, shrugging a little, and turned back to the street. The houses were settled in for the evening, the occupants either vegetating in front of televisions or visiting the pub. I leaned across to the glove box on the passenger side, and I noticed Salma didn't flinch back as I leaned closer. I pulled out a pack of ginger biscuits and the first few CDs I could lay my hand on, and then I opened up the pack and offered it to her. She took three and leaned into her seat, pushing her legs out in a stretch.

"No shitty music, please."

I handed her the CDs, and she rolled her eyes at each of them before dropping them into the space between us. I slipped a Hold Steady CD into the machine, and she smirked as the music started up, so I turned it down low.

"Are these supposed to be songs? He's just talking."

I nodded but didn't rise to the bait. I chewed through a couple of biscuits as the street failed to break into any kind of life. I thought about Gaines for a while, and how she seemed to reach into every corner of my life. She had me, Laura, and Salma all in her pocket. It was getting crowded in there.

And then there was Channy, who I'd made a deal with. Through it all, he seemed to be the only person who wasn't lying to me. The only person playing me straight. My line of thought was taking me nowhere good. I was just sitting in a car snacking on biscuits to a good CD. So why were my nerves burning down to frayed edges? Maybe I needed someone to talk to.

Then I realized Salma had been talking to me.

I tuned in just as she wrapped up. "You weren't listening to a word I said, were you?"

"Sorry, I was thinking."

"You're one of those, huh? Have to stop everything else so that you can get some thinking done."

"That obvious?"

She shrugged. "Seen it before. My husband was the same way. He'd go off for ages. You could watch the light in his eyes come and go."

"How long were you together?"

When she answered, it was with the bittersweet smile of someone who'd come to terms with the divorce, with the realization that you'd both had and lost something special. "Three years. Well, just under. Two years and about eight months."

"And how long you been divorced?"

"A year last week."

Never ask a divorcée what happened to the marriage. It's like a golden rule. Because that question can have only one answer: it ended. Ask them about the good things, the things that will help time and memory wallpaper over the wounds.

I turned to her. "What was he like?"

"Nice guy. Still is. Nice enough, I mean. The legal stuff, the negotiations, that always messes things up, innit? But apart from that, you know. He made me laugh."

"Bet he had bad taste in music though, right?"

She laughed, one of those that comes with a sound at the end of it like it's going to keep going. "Is that bad to me, or bad to you?"

"Both, I'm guessing."

"He liked Brit-pop. Oasis, you know, all that."

I put up a hand. "Say no more. You're better off out of it."

"Danny was—" Whatever she'd been about to say died away when she caught something in my eyes at mention of the name. "You thought I'd married a Muslim, right?"

"Yeah, sorry."

"No biggie. People usually assume. But no, he was white. And I don't mean like you. I mean, like, Danny was *white*."

"He liked Coldplay, too, didn't he?"

The other end of that laugh finally turned up. "Leave him alone. He was sweet, he just—" She paused and then straightened out. "Nothing."

"Okay."

I turned back to the street, watching as the lights in Rakeela's house blinked on and off as someone moved around. It looked like someone had left the living room, gone upstairs to the bathroom, and back down. Whoever was holding the purse strings in the house had people well drilled; turn off lights when you're not using them.

Salma started again. The woman just wanted to talk now, and I was the guy in the seat. People assume I'm a good listener because I don't talk much. Truth is, usually I don't listen—I tune it out. But tonight I was all ears.

"He was hard work. He meant well a little too much, if you know what I mean."

I shrugged. "No."

"It was like he constantly had to show me that he wasn't racist, like every conversation had to be a speech. You know how people get that way? All that I cared about was that he loved me, he was my husband, and he was great in the sack." She grinned. "The rest of it? Just got tiring."

"And your families?"

"They were okay. The same, really. Both wanted to work overtime to show they were okay with it, but both probably weren't, deep down. I think a lot of families still want their kids to stick to their own. How about you? Your marriage was mixed?"

"The problem was more the mixed-up groom than the mixed marriage." She laughed and I smiled. "Laura is one of life's winners, and I'm not. I think she saw me as a fixer-upper, but the cost got too high."

"She ended it?"

What I said about the golden rule? Clearly doesn't apply to women. They ask shit like this all the time.

"We don't really know. I think we both ended it at different times. It's complicated."

"Sounds like it."

"No, not like that. It's over for real. We just have a few friends in common, we run into each other a lot, and it's like each time we're trying to remember what it was like to be friends, which we were before we shacked up. But we never quite get there. Make sense?"

Her eyes flitted across my face as if trying to read me. Was she the person I could talk to about what was eating at me? I wanted to say yes. But, no. There was something missing. Then her eyes left mine and started to follow something that was moving behind me. I turned to see a car slide past and come to a stop outside Rakeela's house.

Both Salma and I slid down in our seats a little, but the light was out in the car; I was sure we wouldn't be noticed. A young couple got out, a skinny white boy with a shock of bright blond hair and a girl with dark skin and long, shiny black hair who looked older by a couple of years. The girl had to be Rakeela, and I looked over at Salma, who nodded. It was the boy who was catching our attention. It was Robin.

Three for three.

Neither of them paid my car any notice. They were too busy eyeing up the house. They were wary of it. I guessed that her family would not approve of their relationship. Robin put a protective arm around her, and they walked to the house in the dim light of the streetlights. Even from this distance you could see she was self-possessed, not as gawky as Ruth or as shy as Bejna. You could also see that she was nervous. In front of the house they paused by a large hedge. It probably sheltered them from view of anyone inside, though it left them exposed to anyone watching from the road.

They kissed awkwardly. Once. Twice. They lingered in each other's arms for a moment, and then Rakeela walked up to the front door and let herself into the house. Robin went back to his car and started to pull away. I put my hand on the ignition, but Salma touched my knee.

"I still don't think it's him."

"He's three for three," I said. "Did you know he and Rakeela were an item?"

"No. But look at how they interacted. You saw how they touched each other. You can't fake something like that."

I didn't answer. Another car pulled past, and it flipped my brain over. It was the same car from the bridge, the teacher, Pearce. He pulled to a stop a hundred yards farther down and then, after a moment, climbed out of the car, whistling. He looked a little under six feet and tightly wound, like his body was still well-trained and responsive. He hadn't reached the stage yet where he'd have to give up PE and teach geography, like they always seemed to. He was carrying a small plastic bag, which he tossed into a trashbin fixed to the nearest lamppost. Then he turned down a driveway to the house.

I fumbled in my pocket for the paper Becker had given me, and unfolded it. There it was, in black and white, Pearce's address. He lived in this street, just a few doors down from Rakeela.

Three for three again.

And now my gut was finally talking to me.

Something was wrong here.

TWENTY-SEVEN

I dropped Salma back at her car. I could feel a mean mood coming on, my senses at once hungry and dull. I drove back into the city and headed for Legs. I parked round the back of the police station a few streets over. When I'm in a bad mood I go for scoring cheap points, and the idea of parking in plain view of the cops to go to an illegal club was about as cheap as I could get.

This was rush hour for the club. All the legal bars and clubs were closing up and kicking out stragglers, which meant that those in the know would head to Legs. I walked to the bar and stared at the beautifully lit bottles lined up on display. The liquids called to me with their perfect hues of gold, amber, and mahogany brown. Did I want a drink?

Fuck yes.

Would I take one?

No.

The pull of the spirits behind the bar was as much to do with a memory as any thirst. They made me think of Rachel, a friend of mine who was a recovering alcoholic. She'd done her best to bring me back to the real world after I'd left my old life behind, and she would have been the perfect person to talk to.

If only she hadn't left the country because of something I fucked up.

I pushed the booze from my mind and bought a bag of oxy. I popped two and waited. The chill hit me like someone running an ice cube down my spine, and it was followed by the numbness. My frayed nerve endings floated away, and all the issues that were making my brain burn felt extinguished. This shit was as good as any prescription I could get from my doctor, and I never had to argue with a dealer over whether I really needed it.

I walked down the stairs into the strip club. The music was loud and crass, but I wasn't paying too much attention to it. I saw familiar faces from around town, and a few dealers who I knew worked for Gaines. I saw Claire Gaines, Veronica's younger sister, sitting in the corner with her hands down some guy's trousers. Class didn't seem to run in the family. Some of the dancers greeted me by name and asked if I needed anything, but I said I was cool.

Cool.

Then I saw Noah, and my problems fought their way back to the surface. He was stepping out of one of the private booths, arm in arm with one of the most popular dancers, a curvy blonde called Crystal or Candy, something like that. Their fake names were hard to remember. She was one of the ones who went the extra mile during a dance, if you paid in advance. Noah had a lazy grin on his face until he saw me. Then he stepped up and came closer and looked straight into my eyes.

"You high?"

"Just something for my injury, you know."

"Uh-huh."

Candy/Crystal kissed him on the cheek, winked a hello at me, and walked away to the dance floor. Noah pulled me by the elbow into the nearest private booth, closing the curtain behind us.

"What's the deal?" he said.

I started to ask what he meant, but he shrugged away the question and looked into my eyes for a moment.

"Look," he said, "maybe Laura hasn't noticed, or Ronny, or Mum. But this is me, okay?"

"I don't—"

"Bullshit, Eoin. Your injuries were, what? Six months ago?"

"Five."

"Five months. How long have you been topping up the prescription bottle?" When I didn't answer, he carried on. "You don't even know which pain you're treating anymore, do you?"

I sat down on the sofa and stared at my feet for what felt like an age. He sat next to me and waited me out, but when I started to talk it was about the work I was doing for Gaines. I told him about the rapes, about Connolly and Salma. Noah just sat and listened, making small noises of agreement or disgust at the right times.

"So what's your problem? Just figure out which of them is doing it."

"Then what? If I take it to Becker, then the guy will walk because there's no evidence. There's no incentive in the girls going to the cops; they'll just be humiliated or ignored. I could walk into Gaines's office right now, give her the two names, and both guys would disappear by tomorrow morning."

"And that's what she's expecting. Even the priest must know that's the score."

It seemed simple enough. Simple, but not easy. Could I live with what would follow once I handed over those names?

"Listen." Noah touched my knee to bring me back from wherever I'd drifted off to. I hadn't noticed going there. "Sounds like you're not ready yet. Buy yourself some time, try and find some evidence, yeah? Try and find something you can give to Becker."

"And if not?"

"You know where Ronny's office is."

There it was again. *Ronny.* My need to fight for her affection reared up again. "Well, you seem more comfortable here than me; maybe you should be the one doing her dirty work."

"Well, you know, there *is* work going. And from what I hear, you keep turning it down."

"She told you that, huh?"

"Look, don't ask me why, but she really likes you. She trusts you." He shrugged. "You're onto a good thing here, if you stop fucking it up. I won't get in your way."

I asked him what he meant, and he just laughed. "Really? Okay, nothing, never mind. She's hot, though, even if you're pretending you haven't noticed. Her sister, too. You ever met Claire?"

"Couple times."

He just waggled his eyebrows, and we both laughed. Then he put his hand on my shoulder and lowered his tone. "You've got a lot running around in that head of yours. Just sit back and chill out, okay? Whatever it is you're on, enjoy it, but don't take any more."

He stepped out through the curtain. I heard snippets of conversation, and then one of the club's dancers stepped into the booth and smiled at me.

"I'm Mitzie." She spoke with an Eastern European accent. It was the woman from Thorn Lane. She had short dark hair, and her makeup had been applied to accentuate her cheekbones. It worked. Her small frame and curves were covered by a thin red dress. "The boss says you need to relax."

She started to dance, and for just a minute I forgot about immigrants and family and lies. I almost managed to convince myself that I wanted it as she moved in front of me and then leaned in close. I almost managed to believe that I wanted her. But as she undid the straps of her dress and began the shimmy that made it drop to the floor, I knew this wasn't what, or whom, I wanted.

I kissed Mitzie on the cheek and left the booth.

Find more proof? Good idea.

Take another oxy? Great idea.

TWENTY-EIGHT

I wasn't really aware of Sunday starting. There are all those songs about coming down on a Sunday morning. I didn't come down; the world came up to meet me. Everything faded into blurry focus, and it was midday.

I left a voice mail for Becker saying I was ready for his help. And then I decided to talk to the person who would know Robin better than anybody. I remembered that his brother worked as a fireman. I thought back to the man I'd seen in the photographs, and it made sense. I could picture that solid frame in a fireman's uniform, not exactly the heartthrob image that women always seemed to imagine.

The fire station was only a couple streets away from my flat, so I walked. I saw someone messing with the engine of one of the vehicles and took my chance. He was young, not much older than Robin, and he was doing something to the engine that involved a jug of water and a pipe cleaner. That's about as technical as I get.

"Hey, man, Mike around?"

He stopped what he was doing and squinted up at me, trying to judge if I was on the level.

"Mike?"

Shit. Had I known his surname? If I had, I'd forgotten it. I searched for something I could use, something Robin had said.

"Yeah, Polski Mike, you know?"

He smiled and then stooped back to the task at hand. "Oh yeah, Fredo. He's off shift, mate."

"*Fredo?*"

"You know, like in *Lord of the Rings*? Well, Mike's like those hobbits, big fucking hairy feet. You ever seen them? But he's like the idiot version, so he's not Frodo, he's—"

I pretended it was the funniest thing ever. "Yeah, gotcha. I like it. That describes him, all right."

"Don't tell him I told you, will ya?"

"Don't worry," I said, touching my nose, "secret's safe with me."

He looked up at me for a second, realizing he'd not asked the obvious question.

"So, you, uh, you're a friend of Mike's, huh?"

"Right. Name's Eoin. He might have mentioned me?" He shook his head, and I feigned surprise. "Aw, come on. He must have, no? Bastard. Ah well, cheers. I'll swing by his house."

"You'd be better trying his office."

"But you said he was off—"

He smiled and turned back to his work. "His real office. The Bottle."

"Cool, I'll catch him there." I stuck out my hand and asked his name. He told me it was Paul.

The Bottle was Ye Olde Leather Bottle, a great pub hidden away on Church Hill on the same road as Robin's house. It was the kind of pub that's becoming scarce; not on a main road, not a theme pub, and it didn't have a fancy name. It was built in 1510, and it had seen most of the town grow up around it. It still stood as a monument to those times, its exterior white plaster walls supported by blackened timber frames; local legend had it as one of the places Dick Turpin stopped to water his horse on the famous ride from London to York. Inside, the walls were painted in browns and greens, and the only real decorations were photographs of old sports cars and an effigy of Turpin in a hangman's noose hung near the bar. I hadn't been in since the smoking ban, and without the haze of smoke at eye level the place didn't feel quite right.

I spotted Mike straightaway, leaning against the bar and sipping a pint of mild. He looked a little older than he had in the photographs, his neck a little thicker and his hairline a little farther back. His cheeks were flushed from the drink, and his jeans were struggling to hold him in. I smiled at Dek, the barman, and ordered a Coke. Then I slid in next to Mike at the bar.

"Hey, it's Fredo, right?"

He turned to stare at me, his glassy eyes showing that this wasn't his first pint of the day. He looked me up and down with a blank expression. "Do I know you?"

"Oh, sorry, mate." I put my hand out for a shake. "I'm a mate of Paul's, yeah? Met you once before at that party—God, when was it?"

He took my hand and then pretended to recognize me, not that he bothered to make it a good fake. "Pete's birthday, right?" I nodded, and he continued. "Yeah, that was ages ago. Good to see you. How you been, like?"

His northeast accent hadn't dimmed at all like his brother's. It was still full-on, and if it wasn't for the beer slowing him down, I might have missed every other word.

"Good, man, good. Yourself?"

"Aye, not bad. You know how it is." He raised his half-drunk pint. "Day off."

"You guys are crazy, you know that? Running into burning buildings. You're meant to run out of them."

"Oh, aye, well, that's still the plan, like. Run out *after* running in."

We both laughed, and I pointed at his pint to see if he fancied another. He nodded yes, and I asked Dek for a fresh pint. If Mike noticed that I wasn't drinking, he didn't show it. After he'd taken his first sip at the fresh drink, I continued.

"What's your real name, by the way? I'm guessing it's not really Fredo."

"No, that's just some dumb shit the lads came up with. It's Mike, Mike Banaciski. Just call me Mike."

"That Polish?"

"Yeah, my granddad moved over after the war, like. We been stinking up the north ever since."

"So what made you move down here, then? I mean, must be more exciting in Newcastle than round here?"

"It was Durham, actually. But you know how it is, a change is good. Even if you buggers have a silly accent."

"Yours is pretty strange, too."

He raised a toast to that. After another hit of beer, this one a long pull, he answered my question again without any prompting.

"Plus the kid—my brother, Robin? He was getting in a lot of trouble, like, so I wanted to move him away, get a fresh start."

"You looking after him on your own?"

"Aye, our parents both died a few years back. Just the two of us now."

"Sorry to hear that."

He nodded and looked into his drink for a moment. Then his head straightened up, and he peered straight into my eyes. I stepped back, wondering if he'd realized I was scamming him.

"Here," he said. "You're the one was selling the eckies at the party, right?"

What the hell, did I look like a drug dealer? I just shrugged, a nonanswer. The more he thought he recognized me, the better my trick would work, but I didn't want to encourage anything.

"Listen, you got anything? I'm having trouble sleeping, right, and I could do with something to knock me out when I get home."

I shook my head and said I'd quit. He pulled a face that said, *Oh well.*

"But, hey," I said. "Not sleeping? I get that, too. I end up going for walks round town at two in the morning, trying to get tired."

"Sign of a worried mind, me mam used to say."

"That what it is with you?"

"Oh, aye, always." He laughed. "That kid of mine, I swear he'll be the death of me."

"This is Robin, right? What's he doing to you? Staying out all night, bringing girls home, playing loud music?"

"I wish. If it was any of that, I could understand. I mean, I'm a guy, right? Been there, done that. Nah, he's hiding something. Getting just like me old man, bottling things up. Ever since our mam, well—"

He didn't have a chance to become maudlin. The television, high up behind the bar, was showing news footage of another PCP rally. A demonstrator had thrown an egg into Marshall's face as he was doing his meet and greet.

"Too right, too, fucking pigs." Mike jabbed a finger at the screen. "Think they forget we're all immigrants here, aye?"

"I'm guessing he can't count on your vote?"

"The things my granddad went through, and my dad, too, it's a disgrace. I mean, freedom of speech is fair enough, but it feels wrong, you know? Letting people like that talk on. There are people out there who'll believe them."

He looked down into his drink again, and then he seemed to snap out of it. He looked up at me with a grin, raised what was left of his drink, and said, "To Pete." Then he pointed at my half-drunk glass of Coke. "You drinking like a woofter?"

"Driving," I said.

"Ah, come on, you can have one. That's legal."

"I tell you what, next time, yeah?"

I found that part of me meant it. Another time, another place, Mike and I could probably have drunk the pub dry, talking about family and football.

He squinted at me then. "You know, you're not the guy I was thinking of. You sure it was Pete's party?"

I said, "You know, maybe you're right." I told him it must have been somewhere else. He accepted it and ordered himself another drink. I gave him a friendly pat on the back and was going to leave him to it when I noticed something else. On the counter beside him he'd laid out the contents of his pockets. His wallet, his mobile phone, his house keys. Lying beside them was an iPod, but the earbuds weren't the white ones that came with it. They looked new.

I remembered Ruth: *I lost my iPod.* And the earbuds I'd found at the scene.

"That thing any good?" I said.

"This? Don't know how to work it, to be honest. I've borrowed it off Robin. He keeps saying I should get one, so I'm seeing if I use it enough to justify buying one. But it's got all his shitey music on it."

TWENTY-NINE

Becker returned my call as I left the pub, and I jumped straight in with a request for him to do some background checks for me. There was a pause on the line when I could almost hear his eyes roll before he said, "What, are you scared of the Internet or something?"

Scared? No.

We never had gadgets around the house when I was growing up. My father didn't care much for any of them, and my mum was only really interested in record players. So I've never really trusted computers, and I don't like living with them. I can access the Internet through my phone because I have thumbs and a brain, but I don't like reading on the small screen.

I can also operate coffee filter machines and microwaves. But that doesn't mean I want to do it all day long.

Other things I'm not comfortable with include spelling and planning ahead. The local library wasn't open on a Sunday, but then most local libraries were no longer open *at all*. There was one failing Internet café in town, with a closed charity shop on one side and a Chinese takeaway on the other. That's where I headed.

I paid for an hour's use. As I sat at the computer, I realized I had no idea how to spell Robin's last name. I sent Salma a text message, and while I waited for a reply, I got on with other work.

David Kyng didn't bring up much straightaway. There was a cheap-looking website for his business, and a couple of social networking profiles that seemed to be him but which I couldn't view. I cursed Becker. Why had he told me that everything I needed to know about Kyng would be easy to find? There was nothing. Then I noticed that the search engine had an option at the top of the page that suggested other spellings of his last name.

Out of curiosity, I changed the search to David King, and the screen almost collapsed under the weight of the results. The top couple of hits were useless. There was a scientist and a real estate guy. A solicitor. But then it got interesting. Old news stories about arson and football violence. King was apparently infamous, the kind of guy who was mentioned by name in football hooligan memoirs. It was impossible to tell which football team he really supported because he seemed to have attached himself to hooligan firms from every team in the northeast at one point or another, from Newcastle down to Hull. There were no news stories that suggested any kind of race hate, or any affiliations with the Extreme Right. He just seemed to be an angry young fanatic looking for a fight.

A couple photographs showed him as a young man, his body lean and brutal, his head shaved, and his eyes cold and dark. Even though the guy was fat now and the years hadn't been kind to him, there was no mistaking that this young skinhead had grown into David Kyng. He'd change one letter and hoped the past would drop away, but it was clear he still liked looking for fights. I wondered how he'd become attached to the PCP. Maybe because it was a place he could find men angry enough to manipulate.

I typed Paul Pearce's name into the magic box and found very little. He popped up on the usual social networking sites, but the listings were protected. I found a few mentions in local news stories about school-related events, and some schoolgirl had written an entry on her blog where she talked about having a crush on him. So much for secret crushes. I remembered carrying a torch for my French teacher for three years—a torch that only me and my bedsheets had known about. I guess that kind of secrecy is old-fashioned.

Eventually Salma texted me the correct spelling of Robin's last name, and I started looking into his background. A lot of boring teenage trivia popped up: endless blog mentions and message board posts that informed me of his appreciation for metal and Japanese horror movies. I tried a search that combined his name with the town of Durham, where Mike had said they were from, and my page filled up with news stories.

None of them good.

Mike had lied about their parents. One of them, at least. Their father was very much dead; that was certain. He'd been a firefighter and had died in the line of duty while fighting a house blaze fifteen years ago. There were pictures of the grieving widow at the funeral with a baby and a very mixed-up-looking young boy. The images bought back memories for me of surviving caravan fires with my family. But I found nothing to suggest that their mother had died.

I still had plenty of time to kill on my prepaid hour, so I started digging into places I probably shouldn't. I read up on Father Connolly, and I tried his name in combination with the Gaines family. There were a few hits: old public funeral listings, a couple of charity events that linked them. The buzz of my phone startled me, and I saw it was Becker. I packed up and went outside to call him back.

"'Bout time," he answered on the fourth ring. "Where you been?"

"Reading."

"Hell, if you don't want to tell me, I don't care. Listen, I did those background checks you asked for—"

"You never heard of the Internet?"

"Smart arse. You want to know what I've found, or you want to talk about porn? Because that's probably all you know about the Internet."

Fair point.

"Anyway. I looked into your guys. First up, forget the teacher. He's fine. He's got a bit of an ego problem when he gets behind the wheel of a car, likes to go fast and show off. He's got a few fines and tickets pending in the PNC, but there's nothing else on him. He's clean."

"Robin?"

"Yeah, okay, that's more of a thing. There's nothing official, mind you, but we do have a flag file on him."

"What?"

"Yes. I called the guy who opened the file, up north some-where outside of Newcastle—Chester something, sounds French, never heard of it. Anyway, he says that it's all off the record, but Robin's a bit of a problem child. Apparently, he went off the rails when he was in junior school. His mum ran away, left the big brother to raise him. He got into all kinds of trouble at school, but then it got serious and he had to move."

That's what Mike had said, too, in different words.

"What kind of serious are we talking about?"

"Girls. Apparently one of the girls at his school was assaulted—that is, with a capital *R*. Nobody was ever arrested, and she refused to cooperate with the inquiry. Then a coworker at the cinema where he worked weekends. Same story again—no official complaint, no case to build. But the police had a quiet word with his brother, told him to take the problem somewhere else."

"Well, he certainly did that."

He paused again. "This is a start, but we'll need more. What else have you got?"

"Indigestion." I hung up.

THIRTY

The sun had faded away by the time I pulled up and parked on Hobbs Road. I was across from Pearce's house, and in the darkening evening the light from his television was casting a glow. Fast-moving lights and shadows played across the hedge in his front yard.

I slipped in the same CD I'd listened to with Salma, smiling to myself when I remembered her description of the music. I drummed my fingers on the wheel in time with the beat and sang along with the lyrics, mostly getting the words wrong.

I was trying not to think about the issue at hand, but it wasn't working. I couldn't keep the questions out of my head. Finding the guy responsible worked in theory. But once you found him, then what?

Doing the right thing would ruin people's lives. Families would get deported, and some young women would be pressured into talking to the police and going through a humiliating trial and media circus. And that was *if* I found evidence.

I got out of the car and crossed to the trashbin where I'd seen Pearce throw a small plastic bag the night before. Condom? Soiled clothes? Could I get lucky and finish it right here? It was a council bin, a black plastic unit with a hole at the front just big enough to slide in my arm. Metal, plastic, chocolate wrappers, and paper. A few damp things slipped across the back of my hand, and I had to fight off revulsion to press on. My hand closed on a plastic bag, and I pulled it out.

Dog shit.

Great.

Elementary, my dear Watson.

I climbed back into the car and wiped my hands on a disposable napkin from a pack I keep in the glove box. As I put the pack back, I saw Boz's gun, daring me to touch it. I lifted it out and held it between my hands, turning it over a couple of times. It felt more substantial than it had before. I pulled out my phone and found Laura's number without pressing the call button. I stared at it for a moment. I pulled Gaines's business card from my pocket and typed in the number. Then I chickened out for a second time. Before I could worry about what that meant, I saw movement outside Pearce's house. I slipped down low in my seat and watched him stepping out of the front door and down the two shallow concrete steps to the path. The lights were still flickering away in the living room, so somebody was still home. His body language changed as he walked to the street, an extra spring appearing in his step. Up closer, I could see age starting to show on him. His shoulders were pushed back a little too far, as if that sort of posture might disguise that his midsection was beginning to look soft through his tight shirt. One look at a guy doesn't always tell you much, but in this case, it was enough to see that Pearce was vain. Clinging to illusions of a younger age before his body threw him off the edge.

He reached his car and dropped down into the driver's seat.

I slipped the gun back into the glove box and reached for the ignition, but I waited until he was halfway down the street before waking my own car up and following him at a healthy distance.

He was driving fast, and it was a challenge to keep up without attracting attention. Usually, I wouldn't think twice. Few people ever assume they're being followed. But I remembered what Becker had said about Pearce's driving, and I didn't want to risk getting too close and have him think I was looking for a race.

He led me round in a loop, down past the Myvod, then turned right and drove in the direction of the motorway junction and the school where he worked. As he drove on past the school, in the direction of the river, I realized where he was going. I think part of me had known as soon as he'd gotten into the car.

I gambled on my conviction, and at the next junction, I turned the opposite way, speeding up to try and get there before him by a longer route. I wanted to be waiting for him. I thought of the gun in the glove box and the speed I was driving, and I thought, *Please, no traffic police tonight.*

I arrived before he did and pulled to the curb beside the bridge, cruising to a spot away from the streetlight before killing the engine and slipping down in my seat. It was only a few seconds before I heard Pearce's car; the headlamps lit up the street around me as he approached. He pulled right up to the entrance to the bridge and then killed his own engine, sitting there as the darkness wrapped around his car.

I inched my hand toward the glove box, trying not to make any sudden moves that would give me away in the shadows, even in his peripheral vision. I lifted out the gun again.

Why?

I didn't know.

It wanted me to—that was the only thought I had as my hand massaged the grip. It wanted me to lift it. I stared at Pearce's car and almost wished he would stare back, but I knew he wouldn't. I could see his profile, and he was looking straight ahead, toward the bridge.

I caught movement across the road and saw the woman from the other night cross in my direction, once again walking her dog.

She walked past me, and if she'd seen me, she didn't show it. As they neared Pearce's car I thought, *Please be the guy, give me something.*

She paused at the end of the bridge, right in front of Pearce's car, and stooped down to fuss with the dog. The dog sat down on its haunches, and she looped the end if its leash over the metal barrier beside them before turning back to Pearce's car.

She walked around the passenger side and opened the door, the light coming on inside as she did so. She leaned down and stuck her head in the car, saying something I couldn't hear. Then she leaned in, and Pearce met her halfway, kissing her.

I dropped the gun onto the passenger seat. I reached for the ignition, watching as the woman climbed into the car and pulled the door shut behind her. The light inside hadn't been off long before the car was starting to rock on its wheels. I looked at the dog, alone in the cold, and thought of the dog shit in the bin. I wondered if she'd bought the dog only as an excuse to slip out of the house at night, or if he'd been around for longer than that.

Fuck it.

If two married adults wanted an affair, it wasn't my concern.

I turned the key in the ignition and got a childish thrill out of the look of shock on the faces of the half-naked lovers as I drove past them. I slipped a few pills into my mouth with my free hand and swallowed them dry.

A chill dripped down my spine, from the tip to the base, and the world felt lighter. My problems drifted away on a cloud.

THIRTY-ONE

"Hey."

I came to as Noah shook me gently. I was in the front seat of my car, right outside the flat. Sunlight hit me in the eyes. I didn't remember driving home.

I rubbed my eyes, shaking my head a couple of times. "I, uh, Monday?"

"We're going to have to have a talk," he said. "Before this goes too far."

I followed him into the flat and showered while he made a pot of coffee. Noah had a certain way with coffee—he laced it with cayenne pepper and cinnamon—and it was the perfect tonic for any occasion.

We settled into the sofa in the living room and looked at each other for a long time.

"You look like hell," he said.

"Thanks, it runs in the family."

"You need to stop. Really."

I changed the subject. "What's the real reason you're back?"

He smiled, clearly indulging me and my desire to steer clear of the obvious. "It's just time, I guess," he said. "I'm older. All the stuff Dai used to say? Family, a woman, working—it all makes more sense now than it did before, you know?"

"I never thought I'd hear you say that."

"Neither did I." He shrugged. "Thing is, it's all the same."

"What do you mean?"

"Settle, travel, whatever. It's all the same trap. That song we were talking about the other night, 'Born to Run,' it's a lie, man. I tried all that, and it hasn't stopped me from being an alcoholic, has it? Hasn't stopped me from gambling or being a prick."

"Too true."

"I just wanted to come home."

"But you didn't go home. You came here."

"Yeah, well. The stuff with Mum, you know, I couldn't stay there. Plus that madwoman across the road."

"Mrs. Daniels?"

"Yeah. I swear, she never remembers me. She thinks I'm breaking in every time I visit."

"She's just old. Things stopped making sense for her a few years ago, but she's harmless. Anyway, she likes me, so maybe she's just a good judge of character."

Then he asked how I was getting on with finding the proof that I needed, and I began to unload. I told him I knew who'd done it. I'd gotten there ass-backward, but a process of elimination left only one option. I laid out the options. It felt good having a big brother again, so I continued. I talked about Laura, about our failed relationship and her being crooked. I don't know how long I talked, but when I finally finished, the coffee was stone cold. Noah took my cup and fetched a warm replacement from the kitchen, and then he settled back down.

"Feel better?"

"I don't know. I think so. I still don't know what to do, though."

We fell silent while we sipped at the coffee. I felt a buried thought tugging at me, as if my subconscious was trying to coax me into remembering something important, but it was like a rope that kept slipping out of my hands. The roar of the caffeine was making my head pound, and I could feel my gut coming alive. I let it drop.

Noah picked up a book off the coffee table, the collection of stage plays our dad had forced on him. "There's this bit I got to. A kid, this is back in Ireland in the 1920s, this kid lost his arm fighting the Brits. In the play he keeps shouting about principles, using them as reasons not to do things. And his mum, I think it's his mum"—he flicked to the page to check—"she says to him that he lost his best principle when he lost his right arm."

"So?"

"Look, I don't know. I had a thought, and then I lost it. All I'm thinking is, you've still got both arms. So it's probably simpler than you think." When I shook my head and laughed, he shrugged. "So what would you rather do? Listen to some of your depressing music, like Ned's Atomic whatsit, or Billy Bogg?"

"Bragg. Billy Bragg."

He grinned at me, and I knew I'd walked into that one. "Noah, none of my music is—well, okay, *some* of it is depressing. But even then, I find that uplifting, like a reaffirmation."

He shook his head. I waved for him to follow me, and I led him upstairs to my music room. We sat on the floor opposite each other and began looking through my vinyl and CD collections. I handpicked albums I thought he might understand and played them one by one. I started with Billy Bragg singing about beaches and love, and Noah almost seemed to get it. I tried to explain how Paul Westerberg singing about loneliness was uplifting, and I played him a couple of examples, but he only connected with the ones that were about drinking. I gave up on the Wonderstuff because he only wanted to hear the one that Vic Reeves swore on. Eventually I left him up there in disgust and went downstairs to make another coffee.

It wasn't until I was standing alone in the kitchen that I again felt as if a buried thought was trying to fight its way to the surface.

Some piece of knowledge was hovering just out of reach. I pushed the feeling away and carried fresh drinks up to the room. Noah grinned up at me.

"What *is* this song?"

I stopped and listened to what was playing. "It's called 'The Road.' It's by Frank Turner. He's good, sort of folk punk."

"It's great." I'd never seen him this enthused about my music. "Really."

The track ended, and the next one started to play. Noah asked me to hit repeat, and we listened to the song again.

"It's our song, man. Listen to it. It's about us. Now, this bit"— he turned the volume up—"it's our song, Smudge. I'm telling you. It's like we wrote it."

Passion, drums, and guitars. Life packed into a song. Words about being shackled to the road, about chasing the horizon and calling it home. Listening to the song with Noah gave it a new life for me. It felt free and real. It felt close enough to touch. I reached out to fully hold the emotion, but instead I grasped the buried thought that had been submerged in my head. I stared down into the coffee in my hand, spiced with cinnamon and pepper. Something perfectly obvious fell into place. Part of me had known the answer all along.

The coffee at Mum's house after the attack, with the strange smell.

Mrs. Daniels never remembering Noah, never liking him.

Oh, you know, he's just a bad one, him. Has that look about him.

You owe us, you Gypsy fuck.

The two guys in hoodies who'd attacked me outside the flat with cricket bats and threats. I felt my teeth ache at the memory. I'd assumed it was a message from Channy Mann, but all at once, I realized it wasn't.

I turned back to Noah. "When you showed up here the other day, you said you'd sat in our bedroom the night before, right?"

He looked at me and shook his head to say maybe, yeah. That put him at Mum's house the night *before* the attack.

"How's the gambling going?"

"What?"

"Those hoodies were after you, not me."

We made eye contact, and in that moment we both caught it. He knew I'd figured it out. There was a moment where we were both frozen; it felt like the music had paused too, like the whole world had stopped.

And then there was movement. He stood and bolted for the door, trying to get past me before I moved. I swung my hand and felt the coffee mug crack as it connected with his face, the hot liquid spilling over both of us. He shouted in pain as he wiped the pepper from his eyes, and I smashed my other fist hard into his nose. He fell back into a pile of CDs, and I followed up with a kick.

There was an animal snarl, and I wasn't sure if it was his or mine, but he rebounded off the floor and dived into me hard. We slammed into the doorframe with a force that shook the thin wall, and then we hit the floor and paused for breath, staring at each other. The music had moved on. Springsteen was singing about a failing marriage, a relationship caught in recrimination and isolation. Caught between the cracks.

I broke the silence. "You ran up some debts?"

He nodded.

"Dai wouldn't keep propping up your mistakes, so you came to Mum for help."

He shrugged, but it was the same as a nod.

"And she went to Kyng for a loan. What happened, did you come back and ask for more?"

"The Taylor brothers in Leeds. I'm into them for six."

"Christ. Six? So you asked for more, and she said no. She was still paying off the last one." He didn't need to nod or shrug this time. "You came round to beg. You got on your knees and made big promises about quitting. But she said no, and you lost it. Did it feel big, hitting her? Did you like how her head bounced off that kitchen door?"

"I try, Smudge. I try to be someone else. I try to be clean and sober. I try not to be a prick. But there's always this anger. There's always—well, we can't help who we are, can we?"

I wanted to be angry. I wanted to find the rage to rip him apart. But it just wasn't there. He looked just as drained. He seemed to crumple inward, as though his pride had been a supporting wall that had just been demolished.

"That's why she wanted to brush all this under the carpet. It's why she called Laura instead of me or Rosie, or even an ambulance."

He breathed out. It was long, and I realized he had been holding his breath since the last time he'd spoken. "That's why I've been staying here. Those first few nights, I couldn't face her."

"But now you can?"

"Well, she's our mum, you know. She said I'm still her son." The dam burst and tears rolled down his face. My cheeks felt warm, and I realized I was crying too.

"It's what mothers do," I said.

"And brothers?"

I searched for an answer. "I don't know."

The flames are finally doing their job. The pub won't be saved this time. It's been years since my parents moved on. Years since the fire in their marriage burned out. All that's left is an empty old pub, me, and my brother.

He knew I'd find him. He'd been doing insurance fraud for months, giving me sideways clues, practically throwing it in my face. It's a test to see if I'm true to my uniform. His only question is whether I'm here to do my job or be his brother?

Never big on subtlety, my brother, he's burning down the home we grew up in. He has me pressed against the wall of our old bedroom. His forearm pressed into my throat.

The fire is loud. It's filling my ears, deafening me. Even with all the noise, though, I can still hear Noah as he threatens me.

He's calling me a pig, a traitor. He's saying I've turned my back on my family, on our history. He's saying I need to choose. I headbutt him, reverse his hold until I have him by the throat, and then I smash his face with my fist. I'm fighting to control my temper. I'm threatening to kill him. I'm sounding like my father.

Once I get him outside, we can hear the sirens—both police and fire service. They'll be on us in seconds. What am I here for?

I swear at him. Punch him again.

Then I tell him to run.

I watch him go.

THIRTY-TWO

Once again, I watched my big brother go. We didn't say anything as he picked himself up and left the flat. I sat and stared at the wreckage. Tidying the room would be easy. But my family? I didn't even know if it was worth the effort.

The only sure thing was that I was too caffeinated to stay in one place for long. I decided to put my energy into the problem that I *could* fix. I pulled on a jacket and stepped outside. I pulled the gun from the glove box of my car and walked the ten minutes to Robin's house.

He answered the door almost as soon as I rang the bell. He had a half-eaten Pot Noodle in his hand, and I could hear a sit-com's canned laughter coming from the television inside. It took him a second to place me, and while he started to piece together a question, I pulled my jacket to one side, to show the gun.

"I'm here about Rakeela."

"What—"

I stepped forward into the doorway, and all of his bravado slipped away. He stepped back into the room, and I followed. Robin stood nervously beside me, not knowing the socially acceptable thing to do when a man threatens you with a gun. I didn't know either; we were both new to this.

"Ignore the gun," I said, defeating the point of having it. "Cheap stunt to get your attention. To be honest? It's not even mine."

His jaw unclenched, and he seemed to relax into a more confident stance, feeling like the king of his home once again. I didn't want to give him time to get too relaxed.

"So, anyway. That stuff we told you before about security? That was bullshit. I've been hired to find the man who raped your girlfriend."

There was nothing subtle about the way I said it. I wanted to gauge his reaction to the word *rape*. He just shook his head, looking around the room as though he'd taken a blow to the head. I tried a softer approach now that the damage was done.

"There's more, too. Two others. Ruth and Bejna. You know both of them, right?" He nodded, but it was a hollow gesture. I couldn't read his facial expression. "Did you know they're both in love with you, by the way? Or whatever love is at their age."

He shrugged, still processing everything I'd said. "Yeah. They both asked me out. But me and Rakeela—well, that's what I wanted."

I felt bad, felt the urge to let up, but I had to keep up with the questions, watch his reactions, see what he knew. "She's pretty, and she looks more grown up than the other two, anyway. More together?"

He sat down on the sofa.

"Can't be easy, though. What does her family think?"

"They don't even know yet. They've met me through the charity group. But Raki's parents hate me, think I'm a dosser. So they don't know about—well, you know."

"Yeah. I've been that guy a few times."

He just looked at me and nodded, his eyes blank, lost. He hadn't committed these crimes. I'd known that when I walked in, but I'd had an anger that needed to be taken out, and he'd been the first person to come along.

"Where's Mike, by the way?"

"Gone down the road for another pint," he answered before thinking. Then, "Why?"

"Why did the two of you move down here? He had a good job, right?"

"Yeah, he loved it."

Slowly I could see the wall going up. He was going to realize where we were headed, and that would be when I'd find out what kind of a man he was going to become.

"So why move down here?"

"No, no. Look, I know what you're—"

"Did it never strike you as strange, all the things that kept happening around you? Your school, your work? Or did you know, deep down? Did you cover for him? Is that what brothers are meant to do?"

I stood up. He didn't make a move.

"His room's just upstairs, yeah?"

I turned and opened the door behind me, the one that led to the staircase. Robin burst into life then and made a grab for my arm. There were tears in his eyes, and his cheeks were flushed red. I pushed him away with the heel of my fist, and he slammed back down into his seat.

I pulled on a pair of gloves as I walked upstairs and looked into the door to my left. There was Robin's damp towel on the floor and the smell of freshly sprayed deodorant. There were an assortment of photographs pinned to the wall, of Robin and the girls. At the cinema, at a theme park, sitting on a bed grinning vacantly. I turned to the back bedroom as Robin ran up the stairs after me.

"You're wrong. That, the thing back home, it wasn't—"

I ignored him and stepped into the bedroom. It was much the same as the living room, sparse but piled high with DVDs and video games. There were a few posters on the wall taken from men's magazines and a Newcastle United football shirt draped on the end of the bed. The smell of cigarette smoke hung thick in the air.

"See, there's nothing here."

I nodded as though I was agreeing with him while I checked out the rest of the room. Aside from the bed, there was no furniture, just piles. A pile of clean clothes, a pile of dirty ones. A box full of deodorants and aftershaves. I felt under the bed, but there was nothing but a mess of clothes and papers. I looked through his clothes, his DVDs. I didn't know what I was looking for until I found it.

A sports bag dumped in a corner of the room.

I opened it up and tipped the contents out onto the bed. Pieces of women's clothing that smelled as though they had been worn. A pile of photographs on cheap paper that I guessed he'd made himself at home with a color printer. The pictures were of women and girls who didn't seem to know they were being photographed. Most were from the street or in a pub: blurry photos taken in a hurry. I turned to the next photo and felt sick. The angle made it impossible to tell which girl he was with, but he'd clearly held the camera at arm's length and posed. The black mask covered his features. Everything except his grin.

Smile for the camera.

The picture quality was the same as the others, but the image wasn't quite the same. It looked like a still from a video clip— it just had that quality of movement that doesn't exist in normal photographs. I suddenly thought of the stash of video clips he likely had on his mobile phone and realized I didn't want to be the one who went through them. I dropped everything back onto the bed, and for good measure I slipped Ruth's iPod earbuds out of my pocket and dropped them on the bed, too.

Robin looked over my shoulder at all the evidence. His fists were clenched, and he looked like a bottle rocket ready to explode. The color of his face was changing from the red of defensiveness to the white heat of adrenaline-fueled rage. I heard the front door open downstairs and the sound of some classic rock song being murdered through a tuneless whistle. Robin heard it too, and he exploded into action, like a bottle rocket set alight. He turned and burst from the room.

I followed, but not fast enough. I could already hear a dull thudding noise as I reached the stairs. When I reached the living room, Mike Banaciski was curled in a damaged ball just inside the front doorway, and his younger brother was all over him like a wild animal.

I tried to pull Robin back, but he was driven by the animal strength that had been unleashed inside him. I heard something crack as his fist drove into his brother's face again, and this time I found enough muscle to drag him away. I pulled just as his own momentum was in my favor, and he fell backward across the room, nearly sending me tumbling in the process. He turned to me as if about to attack, and in that moment I saw nothing human in his eyes. As he coiled for another leap, I pulled Boz's gun out and pointed it right at him. I hoped that I looked like a tough guy and not someone who was scared shitless. I must have managed to hold the gun convincingly because I saw the white heat fade from his face. His eyes softened, and he looked human again.

He nodded to show me he was calm enough, and I turned to his brother. Mike laughed, but it came out as a gurgle. Air bubbles formed in the blood around his smashed nose, and a wheeze followed as he tried to take a breath. One of his eyes was already vanishing beneath the swelling.

"What're you laughing at?"

"You." It came out sounding like "*mniew.*"

"Why did you do it?"

"Because I want to, and because I *can*. Nobody cares. If they did, they'd have stopped me back home, the first time, not just covered it up and asked me to move."

My stomach turned over. "With the evidence I've got now, the police would be all over you."

He laughed again, a wet and sickly noise. "*Mngight.* Do that, and I'll ruin them. All of them. The illegals? The old man? Salma? I'll bring them all down with me."

I looked down at him over the gun. He was right. Turn him in, and the whole thing would be pointless. The girls would be ruined, and the illegals would be deported.

I stepped in closer to make sure he could see the gun with his one useable eye. I noticed as I did that his collarbone was at a funny angle.

Another brother.

Another liar.

My breathing stopped, and my heart felt like it was going to pound right out of my chest. I stepped in closer and tightened my grip on the gun.

"Do I look like I'm going to turn you in?" I said.

THIRTY-THREE

"You did the right thing."

"I'm not sure what the right thing is these days."

"Well," Father Connolly said as he leaned back and looked up at the altar, "whatever it is, I think you did it."

I'd called him after leaving Robin's house, and he'd agreed to meet me at the church. I talked at him for a long time. I guess you could say he took my confession. I told him about my family and my fight with Noah. Then I told him about Mike and holding the gun on him.

The power it had given me.

Then I told him how I'd called Becker and handed Mike over to the cops, even though I didn't quite know what they would or could do with him. That was when Connolly had told me I'd done the right thing.

"He'll talk. You know that?" I said. "Mike, I mean. He'll tell them all about the charity, what it really does. The cops will have to come for you and Salma."

He chuckled, but it turned into a brief cough. "Let them come. If they want to arrest a sick old man for giving people food and shelter, they can try. I don't think they'll get very far."

"But Salma?"

"She made her choice. We all did."

"You knew what Gaines was doing with some of them, right?"

I would have expected him to avoid my eyes, but he met me dead-on.

"She gave them jobs and a home. Some of those jobs were not"—he winced, trying to find the right word—"*ideal*. But they were jobs. I'm just doing the best I can. Like you, I would say."

Ouch.

"The case is still difficult. Becker's working it, but it's touch and go. There's video on his phone that could be used to make a case that he's raped a number of girls, but if none of them are coming forward...And so far he's not confessing to anything."

"But surely that is proof enough?"

"Well, at this stage it's not about whether there is proof that would stand up in court; it's about whether there is proof that will get it taken *to* court. The police gather evidence and file paperwork, but it's the Crown Prosecution Service that will decide if the case goes any further. It's almost like an audition. The more holes there are, the more a defense lawyer can do, and that makes the CPS twitchy."

"So he could get away with it."

"I'm no lawyer. I don't really know how it will work out. But no victim and no confession? Yeah, I'd say he could get away with it. What then, Father? What if he turns up at your door, looking for forgiveness?"

He shrugged. "It's what I'm here to do. What's the alternative? The girls come forward and the media eats them alive—at least until the illegal ones are sent packing?"

"Yes. Or he cuts a deal, uses what he knows about the immigrants to get off. The cops are big on that kind of thing right now."

"You think we should move them?"

"I think that's Gaines's problem. She's got people in the police who'll tell her the moment he starts giving anything up."

He nodded again. "How close did you come? Were you going to pull that trigger?"

"Maybe I should have, you know? I keep thinking that."

He sat back and smiled. It wasn't a happy smile, but it was comfortable. He seemed at peace with what had happened. "I didn't make any big speeches when you first came in here. I don't really believe in them, to be honest. But there is one thing I believe in that's worth saying: I believe in God. I believe he's up there. But down here it's just us, and we have to show some responsibility."

"We're not very good at it."

"No, we're not. People come in here looking for things I can't give them. Forget the sermons. You don't earn redemption in one act or one prayer. Doing the right thing once isn't enough. You have to keep doing it. That's what gets you there."

I unfolded a news story I'd printed off at the Internet café and passed it to Connolly. He scanned it and nodded. Then he handed it back to me.

"I shouldn't be surprised, really, that someone like you found that out."

"What happened?"

He started to talk, and I wondered if anyone had ever heard his confession. Who listens to the guy who always listens?

"I was a lot like you when I was younger. Except I had maybe more places to direct my anger. This was back when there were the pub bombings, the blackouts. Anyone with my accent, or my parents' accent, could get arrested and beaten. It made it very easy to be angry."

I looked again at his large hands and pictured him in a different light, as an angry young man with strong fists.

"Sounds familiar."

He held my look for a moment before drifting off into whatever part of him held the memory. "My family goes back a long way with the Gaines clan. Ransford and I were practically brothers. I ran with him, worked with him. I did things I'd rather forget."

"What changed?"

A shrug. "*I* did. The anger was burning me up. I realized it would kill me if I couldn't make some kind of peace with myself. So I followed my family's other tradition."

"And after you took your vows—"

"Yes, they came to me. I heard confessions. I gave advice. I heard so many things—that family trusted me with so much." He laughed. "It would make a hell of a memoir."

"So the girl who was raped?"

"Was Ransford's older sister, Veronica. She came to me for advice, and I gave it. I stayed quiet, didn't tell anyone. Sometimes I pretend it was because of my vows or some moral code. Really, I was just scared of their old man. Michael Gaines was a scary son of a bitch. And I used every excuse I could not to confront him or report him. I was a coward." He hung his head. "You become a prisoner to something like that. It starts to define who you are. It changed me."

"You never told anyone."

"Veronica never recovered. In and out of hospitals, homes. Hidden away from the world. She took her own life. She was about twenty-two, I think. She'd been on medication for years, and she'd had enough. She was already gone by the time Ransford found her."

He'd named his eldest daughter after his dead sister. It was almost sweet.

"After the funeral, I confronted the old man. I threatened to kill him. I talked about God and judgment and all of that. I used all of my anger up, I think, in that one go."

He paused with a faraway look as if dusting cobwebs from old memories, and I unfolded the news story again and reread it to give him the chance to collect his thoughts. He paused for a cough.

"Was it you?"

"No, I didn't kill him. I'd made all those threats, but I didn't have it in me to follow through on any of them. I was an angry young man, you know, but I was still scared."

Did I ever.

I'd picked out a fresh detail as I'd reread it, and now I was curious. "When they found him, he had a coin pressed into his mouth. Did that mean anything to you?"

He laughed. "The police asked me if that was my little Judas joke. They really can be idiots sometimes. But no, it didn't mean anything."

"So the police treated you like a suspect. Why?"

"Witnesses had heard me threatening him. I wouldn't tell them why because I still felt I had to protect Veronica's trust, but they pushed me hard."

"But you didn't know who'd done it?"

"I realized it didn't matter. Not to me, anyway. My anger had gone, and the saddest part of the story was over. I didn't need to know everything about everybody anymore. Two people were dead, but there were a lot of other people left alive, and I had work to do. I think that was when I grew up."

He'd evaded my question a little bit. I decided it didn't matter because I had a more burning question. "You knew my father?"

"A troubled man. I see so much of you in him."

"Tell me about him."

"No. I think that's a conversation the two of you should have." He coughed again, bent double this time and bringing up something cold and wet with it. He sat drawing in deep breaths after he'd finished, and relaxed a white-knuckle grip on the bench. "Both of you have so much anger. You've got to make peace with who you are. Otherwise, you'll be carrying this anger around until the day you die. Believe me, I've seen it."

THIRTY-FOUR

Make peace with who you are.

I drove around for the best part of an hour. I half listened as Tom Waits sang about getting behind the mule and I let the low-key rumble wallpaper my tired brain. I must have known where I was driving to, but I didn't admit it to myself until I was there.

Channy Mann answered on the fifth ring. He lived with his wife and children in a decent-sized house in Marlborough Gardens. It was a quiet estate made up of three- and four-bedroom houses; these were homes for teachers and middle managers, not criminals. It backed onto a private tennis club and was across the road from the Wolves' private training ground.

Like most of the middle-class areas in the Black Country, the estate was an island. If you took a wrong turn at the end of any of the estate's roads, the money started to drop away. Five minutes farther on and you'd be heading into immigrant central. Poverty and privilege have always lived next to each other in the Midlands.

Mann opened the door wearing a robe over faded pajamas. The house behind him was in total darkness as he stood in the doorway. He brushed sleep from his eyes and asked me what I wanted. I said I needed to talk, and he stepped aside, waving me in. He pointed me to a door at the back of the dark hallway. I walked past the wall of family portraits and a bag of golf clubs and pushed through the door. It opened onto the kitchen, and Channy switched the lights on as he stepped in after me. The room was large, divided in two by a handsome kitchen island topped by a thick wooden counter. On one side was the kitchen itself, gleaming with modern appliances. To the other side was an open dining area. A child's schoolwork lay open on the table.

Channy waved for me to pull up a stool at the kitchen island. I slid into the seat and leaned on the counter, still feeling numb. He opened the cupboard above the sink and pulled out a bottle of Jameson and two tumblers. The bottle was already half empty. He unscrewed the top and pointed the end at me. I shook my head, and he put one of the tumblers back in the cupboard before taking a seat opposite me. He poured himself a large measure. Some of the whiskey spilled over the edge of the glass as he poured, and the sharp, beautiful smell of it wafted up to my nose.

"It's late," he said.

"Sorry if I woke your family up."

He shrugged. "It's my house. If I want to talk to someone, I'll talk to someone."

Right.

As a man with a failed marriage behind him, I could recognize a defensiveness in his voice, a tone I'd hidden behind on many an occasion early on. I wondered if there was anybody sleeping upstairs and how long that homework had been sitting on the table.

"Nice house."

"You've been here before, when you first started working for us."

"Gav talked to me in the garage. I never came into the house itself. It's not what I was expecting, somehow."

"What was that?"

"I don't know. Bigger, more showy. Something a bit more *Scarface* or *Godfather*, you know what I mean?"

"I love both those films, I've got them in the living room, but I wouldn't want to live in them. You have to know what you want. Do you want to be rich, or do you want to be *seen* to be rich? You've seen that big house that old man Gaines lives in? It's almost a palace, innit. Me? I'm simple. I just want a warm place and some nice clothes. Money goes further if you don't spend it."

"Makes sense."

He sipped at the whiskey and then stared at me for a long time. I could hear the fridge humming. I saw a pile of unwashed dishes in the sink. Each carried traces of a different meal. A man eating alone over a number of days.

"Yes, it does. When my parents came to this country from Bangalore, the white people didn't want them around. Didn't want to talk to them or live with them. They said we smelled funny. Politicians said there would be rivers of blood. The guy who said that, he was talking about us here, you know? He was the local MP; he meant our streets. Fifty years ago my dad couldn't get a job in West Brom. Now? I make one call and a thousand people in West Brom lose their jobs. You see it? Now politicians come to me for donations."

"Living the dream." There was a sneer in my words. He picked up on it straightaway and stared the sarcasm out of me with his eyes; the whites of them were yellowed and crisscrossed with veins from too much stress and alcohol.

"People like us—me, Gaines—you know where we start? Our communities. Our families come over from somewhere else, and they get attacked. They need protection, so we get organized. Then ten, twenty years go by and, shit, *I'm* the man."

"I've seen some of the Birmingham gangs hanging around your spots. The reds and purples—which ones are they? Watsons? The Meatpackers?"

He nodded. "Those are old names. The world's changing, you feel it? My day it was about community. Those riots—kids just angry, just fighting, and for what? They've never been spat at, never been burned out or knocked down. You seen it, right?"

Seen it? I'd been in it. "Yes."

"We kept Birmingham out of this town for twenty years, but it's different now. When the cops put the Watsons away, it was like small crews of guys came from everywhere to take their own bit. Each crew has its colors and its code, or so they think. And now they're coming to take ours."

"And you're jumping into bed with them?"

"Survival."

This didn't sound like the Channy I knew. He'd always been more respectful of the old ways of doing things. His was a generation raised on Scorsese movies and respect. There was a moral code and a hierarchy. Now he was talking like he'd let any dumb kid from the street get right into the game. I told him he'd changed.

"Well, you changed me, eh? You and Gaines. Gav was always the loud one, the fighter. I was the thinker, the planner. I always thought I held Gav back, kept him in line, but now I think he held me to a certain standard."

I looked again at the signs he was living alone. And at the madness eating away at the corners of his eyes. He was waiting to explode, and I didn't want to be around when it happened.

"I'm done, Channy. I'm not like you or Gaines. I want out."

After a moment he nodded and refilled his glass. "You know how you can get what you want."

"This thing with Vero—with Gaines. I give her to you. I want all my debts cleared. No more obligations or games. Yeah?"

He smiled without a single trace of pleasure. He said yes. Do this thing for him, and I could walk away. He sounded like he meant it. I said I was serious, and he pointed to the ceiling.

"I swear on my children," he said.

I shrugged and then stood up.

"Be ready the next time I call," I said.

THIRTY-FIVE

I woke up around three the following afternoon. After meeting Channy I had driven around the Black Country for a few hours, listening to music and letting it soften the hard edges of my thoughts. At some point, I'd pulled around the front of my flat. I'd had just enough energy to get up the stairs to my bedroom before I lay down and the world went white.

I dreamed of women: Gaines. Laura. Salma.

I dreamed of family: Mum. Dad. Rosie. *Him.*

I couldn't tell if it was pain or the weight of obligation that woke me up, but I felt something crawling through my guts like a snake. The flat seemed cold and empty now that I was alone again. I showered and took a few pills, and for a moment the water of the shower hung in the air around me.

I popped another pill and cooked the largest plate of fried food in history. Then I let it go cold as I sat and stared at a space on the wall for almost an hour. Somewhere along the way my phone beeped and told me I had a voice mail. It was from Boz. He wanted help filling in a job application form. I added that to my list of things to get to. The list that only ever got longer.

To prove me right, the door buzzer sounded right on cue. I pressed the button without asking for a name, and a minute later, Rick Marshall stood in my doorway. Even through the fog shrouding my brain I knew I wanted to keep annoying this man.

"What's up, Ricky?"

"I, uh. Listen, can I buy you a drink?"

"Nope."

"Don't want to be seen out with the bigot?"

"I don't drink."

"Right." He smiled. "Can I buy you a Coke, then? Somewhere away from the town center?"

"What's on your mind?"

"It's about the illegal immigrants."

What?

It took only about five minutes to drive him to the Myvod.

It was busier than I expected when we walked in. The pool table had been claimed by a gang of underage boys wearing tracksuits and haircuts crisscrossed by tramlines. Some of the men at the bar looked familiar—people I went to school with, I guessed. They all had the same look, prefaded jeans and T-shirts bought from High Street shops, probably by their wives. Hair short and thinning. Eyes glazed by one too many lagers.

We settled into one of the booths farthest from the door with a pint of lager for him and a pint of Pepsi for me. I watched Marshall's face as he took in his surroundings, picked up on the rough laughter, the loud conversations, the thick accents.

"Not from around here, are you?"

He smiled down at his drink and then looked up at me. "That obvious?"

"Your skin might not be crawling, but it's not comfortable. I'm guessing you grew up somewhere with a little more polish?"

"I grew up in Stoke, actually. It's not any better than here."

"No, it's not. But it had a nice part of town, right? Or you lived in the countryside outside Stoke, one of those quiet little villages. A grammar school, maybe? Middle-class kids who knew how to pass an exam at eleven years old. I'm guessing you didn't start to see people of color until you got older and ventured to the next town over for drinks?" He didn't deny it, so I carried on. "Your dad voted Conservative his whole life, got bitter when they let him down. And Labour, of course, was unthinkable."

"Always."

"Is that why you got into politics? Make him proud?"

"I believe the things I say. That's why I'm involved, which is more than you can say for a lot of politicians these days."

"Closed borders, no asylum. Jobs going to white people."

"I never said *white* people. I just want to level the playing field. Look, it's about equality, okay? A friend of mine, highly trained engineer, lost his job because the economy took a dump. Then he couldn't even get a job as a bus driver because they were giving them to any immigrant with two legs. Is that right? Is that fair?"

"Do you ever think what this country would be like without immigration? I don't see the Neanderthals being able to fix pipes or drive buses, do you?"

"You're being silly, going back that far."

"Okay, pick an era. Draw a line in the sand wherever you want, you don't just find white people."

"Look, it's about our banks, our newspapers, our oil companies. They're not owned by us. They're owned by Russians and Americans. The Germans control our savings. The Japanese sell us our cars. We don't build anything anymore. Look at this town. How many tanks did they build here that rolled out to win us a war? How many families were supported by foundries and coal mines? Their sons and daughters have nothing now. This country is being raped."

An anger I didn't know I had in me boiled over. "Don't use that word. You don't fucking know."

He spread out both his hands in a peacemaking gesture. "You're right. Look, I'm not here to get into a political debate. I just think the government shouldn't force us to mix. And I mean that with respect to all sides." I could tell he'd made a conscious effort to avoid saying *us* and *them*. "All this political correctness, positive discrimination—it's taking away British culture. We can all have a share, but most communities seem better off when they stick to their own. I mean, look at the riots—"

"Mostly *Gorjer*, from what I saw."

"*Gorjer?*"

"You lot. White folk."

"Well, I disagree. I saw lots of angry minorities, all wanting a piece. But anyway, I meant what I said to you the other day. About moving my party forward. It's taken a lot—I mean, there are guys out on the right who hate me for it. There are some real crazies out there who think I've betrayed them. I'm just trying to bring us into the middle."

"Where the votes are?"

He shrugged again. "Nothing wrong with that." He fingered the edge of his pint, wiping the moisture from the glass with his thumb. Then he made a decision about whatever was troubling him. "Our people know. About the flats, I mean."

My blood ran cold, and I blinked about half a dozen times. He read my silence and carried on. "We've got a few friends on the force, you know? Not many, but a few."

"So the police know the details?"

"Uh-huh. They've got some fireman in custody for another crime. He's talking about everything except what they've got him for. They say he's trying to talk his way out, and it's working. He's given them a list of places where he fitted smoke alarms for illegals— flats, houses, workplaces. He's given them the flats on Thorn Lane."

"If they know, how come they haven't made a move?"

"This is fresh. A couple hours old, at most."

"And why are you telling me?"

"Leaks like this happen for a reason. If they wanted to cause a stink, it would have been the press who got told, not us. It's gone straight to the racist loonies in the party—Kyng and his lot—and I have to fight to keep them in line as it is."

"Someone's looking for a fight."

"Someone is looking for those rivers of blood."

This was the second time someone had mentioned that "rivers of blood" speech to me lately. I wondered if Enoch Powell had thought it would end up so famous.

"Call the cops. Tell them it's been leaked."

"Right. I call them, they have to follow the rules. They're already following the rules. They'll be seeking clearance to raid the flats right now, and nothing I say to them will speed that up. You're connected. Get them out."

He pulled out a brown envelope. He placed it on the table between us.

"What's that?"

"Tapes. This is a recording of the cop who tipped us off."

"And you just happened to have a tape recorder?"

"No, we record all inbound calls. We get a lot of threats, and we want to be covered if any of them ever follow through."

I put my hand on the package but didn't pull it toward me. I tightened my grip, but then I pushed the package back toward him. "Let the police deal with it," I said. "Give a statement, get people arrested."

He pushed it back. "Political suicide. No way."

Political suicide. The penny dropped. "That's all this is, isn't it? You've known about the flats all along. That's why you've been rallying here, getting ready to play your trump card. But now the game's changed. You leave it to your loonies, and their vigilante violence will destroy your party name a few weeks before an election. You help me get them out, and you get off—hell, you might even benefit. You can shout about how illegal immigrants get everything for free."

He leaned back and folded his arms. "So? Do you care about that right now? It'll be getting dark before six. The people in the flats don't have much time."

THIRTY-SIX

Move.

I didn't stick around to ask if Marshall needed a lift home. I got the car in gear and left the pub with the kind of tire spin that makes every man grin deep down inside. I had the fading March daylight in my favor. Nobody would move until it got dark; the riots had given everyone plenty of practice in this kind of thing.

I called Becker, and he answered straightaway. "What?"

Nice.

"I need your help. Listen, there's a leak. Someone on your side has tipped off Community about the flats and—"

"And I'm on the verge of losing my place on the team because I trusted the wrong fucking gypsy. I've been running PNCs for you, leaving a trail a mile wide to help you catch a rapist, and now it's all gang related. Human fucking trafficking?"

He hung up. I stared at the phone in my hand for a second. Shit, was that one fixable? I knew I should call him straight back, try and talk it out, but I didn't have time. I called Laura, but got her voice mail. I shouted into it, pretty much just key words. I called Gaines and got straight through, though she sounded sleepy. I guess that's what happens if you call a vampire during the day.

"They know."

"What?"

"The police, they know about the flats."

"That's not possible. They would have told me."

"Well, you need to work on your sources. Maybe you've missed a few payments or something. You want to know whom they did tell? Community."

"Shit. Where are you?"

"In my car. I'm on my way to the flats."

"Don't worry. PCP won't move until it gets dark. They'll want cover, and the families will be at work right now anyway. I'll arrange transport for them, but you'll need to get them all rounded up and packed."

"Me? They won't trust me. Most of them won't even understand me. I'll need to get Salma."

"You should have let us deal with the rapist, you know."

Subtext: This is all your fault.

If I'd pulled the trigger, or let Gaines cut a piece off him, then a whole load of people wouldn't be about to lose their homes.

I pulled up outside the flats and watched the youngest children playing football in the car park. I'm not very good at *planning* things; I like to feel things out and make them up as I go. This was not going to be my finest hour. I left voice mails for both Salma and Connolly before I realized the obvious.

I knew someone with all the right connections.

Someone who could maybe get them away from Gaines in the bargain.

I called my little sister.

Rosie turned up soon after, with Mum in tow. She was driving a large, beat-up estate car, and the trunk was piled with blankets and medicine. She was like a small-scale version of the Red Cross. As the adults started arriving home from work, she handed out supplies and talked to each of them in turn. She and Mum listened to everybody's stories, offering smiles, sadness, and sympathy in equal measure. I saw for the first time how similar they were—and how different from me. Noah and I were like our father; Rosie was like our mother. I'd never felt farther from the women in my family than I did in that moment: they were all the things I wasn't.

A few people were standing and watching from the other side of the road. There were no houses or shops over there, nothing but a small industrial estate and a car showroom. They were not locals or passersby. They were watching for a reason. Mum approached me and nodded at them.

"It's about to kick off," she said. Her voice had the weariness of a mother who'd been chased out of any number of homes. "We need to get the police in."

I shook my head. "The minute the police get here, all these people will be rounded up and deported. We need to move them."

"How?"

"Well, either Rosie finds a charity to take them right now, or—"

"Or?"

"Gaines. If we round them up, she can move them."

I watched her chew her bottom lip, swallow a lifetime's worth of anger, and try to make sense of it all. She turned on her heel without a word and went back to work, talking and preparing the families.

Shadows started to fall across the sky as the chilly early spring evening crept in. Rosie touched me on the arm a couple minutes later, told me there was a woman refusing to pack. Somehow I knew it would be Sally even before I heard her name. When we got to the foot of the steps leading up to Sally's flat, Bejna greeted us and shook her head.

"Mama won't leave," she said.

She turned and led us up the steps and in through the front door, and the minute Sally saw us she started to shout, "No, no, not running again!"

I talked as low as I could, trying to sound soothing, but it didn't help. Rosie tried too, but again Sally shouted.

"I run here! This is where we will stay. No more, we are home now!"

Bejna turned us and said, "Let me talk to her."

Rosie and I both nodded and headed to the kitchen to give them a few moments alone. Rosie switched the kettle on out of reflex, and then she noticed what she'd done and laughed. I caught the smell of burning and turned to look at the cooker. There was nothing on, so I dismissed it and turned back.

"Listen, I know about Noah and—"

"What's that noise?"

She'd heard it before I did. The kind of chipping sound that only comes from fire eating into something it shouldn't. I caught the overpowering smell of gasoline and a great heat that was coming from somewhere below us. I heard Mum shout out my name. Then we heard the sound of the living room window smashing in. It was followed by screams and the unmistakable smells of furniture burning and gasoline. Then the world slipped me by for a second.

I've been here before.

THIRTY-SEVEN

Stay still.

This is not happening.

I stayed rooted to the spot. This couldn't be happening again. My life was stuck on a loop. I turned to look at Rosie; her eyes were wide and pleading. She'd never been old enough to know what was going on when we used to get burned out. But this must have been touching some half-remembered fear, just as it was with me. I looked again into Rosie's eyes and thought, *Shit, this one's on me.*

Move.

In a fire you get only seconds. Maybe a couple of minutes, if you're very lucky. After that, the place is a death trap and you're not getting out. I put my arm round Rosie's waist and propelled her through the door into the hallway. Thick black smoke was already coming out of the living room doorway, and with nowhere to go, it was building up in the hall ahead of us. I bent down low, and Rosie followed suit as we inched through the smoke, looking for the door. I heard the whooshing sound of a fire at full burn in the living room. It's a sound you can't mistake for anything else. Hear it once and it's with you for good in your dreams.

The flat was going up fast.

Whoever had made the Molotov cocktails knew what they were doing.

The heat was getting to be too much, rolling out of the living room like a wave. I found the handle, but the cheap metal was hot. The plastic doorframe was starting to warp, so I put my weight into it. I didn't budge. I pulled my sleeve down over my hand and turned the handle and swung the door inward. The smoke now had somewhere to go, and our vision cleared slightly. I pushed Rosie through, into the fresh air, and then I stepped out after her onto the balcony at the top of the stairs. She was leaning over the edge, coughing from somewhere deep inside herself.

I heard Mum call both our names, and I saw she was standing outside one of the ground-floor flats, shepherding people away from the smoke. The people leaving the building didn't have far to go, as the crowd across the road had grown and were advancing, shouting racist chants and telling the people who lived in the flats to go back where they came from.

The immigrants were trapped between the burning flats and the crowd. There was a gap between the two groups, and so far nobody had crossed the line, but it was only a matter of time. I pushed Rosie toward the stairs, where Mum was now waiting for her. I looked across the heads and faces in the crowd, but I couldn't see Sally or Bejna. I'd known I wouldn't, unless they'd gone out a back window, because they hadn't come out with us through the front door. I turned to look back at the open door and the smoke that billowed out, blocking the doorway and bounding out toward me before rising to the sky. It looked like every nightmare I'd ever had, as if the smoke was about to take me.

I could see in through the broken window, but all I could see were the flames. There was the sound of plaster and paper falling from the walls. The top half of the room was lost to a roiling black cloud. I ran the odds in my head, but all I could think of were reasons not to go in.

As I stood there I saw some of the immigrants break away from the crowd and run toward the edge of the car park nearest to me, at the back of the houses. I looked in the direction they were running and saw the people who had thrown the Molotov cocktails. Two of them were big; I was reminded of the hooded thugs who had attacked me. The third was smaller, and he was still holding a cocktail, about ready to throw it. He saw me as I saw him, and even through the balaclava covering his features I knew who he was.

He dropped the bottle at his feet and turned away, running into the darkness at the back of the houses. I thought about giving chase, but then I heard a very human sound from inside the flat. I stepped back to the doorway and dived through the smoke.

What the fuck am I doing?

I ducked low. The smoke roiled above me, and the wallpaper dropped down around me in flaming sheets. I called out Sally's name, followed by Bejna's, but there was no response. I took another breath but then coughed out something black. I decided not to do that again.

I crawled into the living room, ignoring the heat that threatened to suffocate me. The carpet was hot to the touch and curling up as its glue no longer held it to the floor. I didn't fancy being on it when the flames decided to see what it tasted like.

I crawled forward until I found what had once been the sofa. It was now a molten liquid mass, giving off fumes and making my eyes sting. I reached the chair, which was made of different material and burning away like a bonfire. I couldn't get past it, but beyond I could see what had once been a shelving unit, now broken and toppled to the floor. It was smoking but hadn't caught fire.

I turned round, screwed my eyes shut against the smoke, and started back toward the door. Someone grabbed hold of my leg. I couldn't make out who it was in the darkness, but I felt the hand tighten its grip. I reached back and held it, and tugged in the direction I was moving, hoping they would get the message. I crawled on with my weight on one arm, guiding my follower with my other hand.

I tried for the doorway but was forced back by the heat. I opened my eyes long enough to see that the flames had formed a wall and were spreading toward us.

What the fuck am I doing?

The only other option was the window, which I guessed was somewhere to my left. That would mean standing up. It would mean having only seconds to follow through before the heat and the smoke took me down. I turned back and crawled close to the person clutching my leg. It was Sally, and she had an unconscious Bejna hooked beneath her other arm. I didn't know where she was getting the strength.

I barked out the word *window* and hoped she could hear me or lip-read. I pulled up a section of carpet and rose to my feet. I stepped forward until my arms hit the jagged glass around the frame, and I punched away at it from behind the carpet.

I felt my hands tear as the glass tore through the carpet. Then I felt enough glass clear away that I could put weight on the frame.

I climbed over the edge and breathed in fresh air—massive gulps of it that burned my lungs. Then I turned back to see Sally standing in the window, her face obscured by the smoke. I pulled Bejna away from her, taking her full weight slowly, and started down the steps.

I took a couple steps, but then my bad knee buckled, and I toppled forward, leaning into the railing to try and steady myself. Two men ran up the steps and met me, lifting Bejna from me and then guiding me down the steps before they ran back up past me, toward the flat.

Bejna was laid out on the concrete, still unconscious. Two women fussed over her, taking turns to breathe air into her while Rosie stood over them with her mobile phone, holding a hurried conversation with someone on the other end and then relaying instructions to the women. I tried to offer my help, but I broke out into a fit of coughing and felt my knee go again. My stomach heaved as I hit the floor, and I threw up something black and sticky onto the concrete, planting my hands down either side of it to steady myself as the world spun.

I heard a cough, coming like the rattle of an empty can of spray paint, and then a louder one, full throated, and looked up to see Bejna turning onto her side and throwing up black tar of her own.

The men who had steadied me came back down the stairs, walking on either side of Sally, holding her upright. She had a huge gash across her forehead. The blood was congealed along her hairline, and her sleeve was smeared crimson where she must have kept wiping her eyes clear. Her right arm hung limp at her side. She staggered and then dropped to her knees beside her daughter.

As Bejna looked up at her with a weak smile, Sally relaxed, and then she screamed, clutching at her right arm. She'd been carrying Bejna with a dislocated shoulder.

More locals were gathering round us now, but this wasn't a hate mob. People from the nearby houses were bringing blankets and water. Three people near me were talking to emergency services on their mobile phones. Beyond them the Community mob had been pushed back across the road by a row of burly men, with Bull shouting at them to fuck off or step up. Gaines's cavalry had arrived, and they had ridden in on white transit vans to move the families.

Rosie was kneeling on the ground, still holding an urgent phone conversation in between drinking water and coughing. She kept using initials and acronyms, so I figured she was talking to one of her nonprofit people. Sounds were coming to me in bits and pieces as the world around me seemed to speed up and slow down. I heard snatches of shouting and chatter, Bull's voice booming loud. I heard Rosie coughing and, somewhere, sirens. Some sleepy part of my brain was talking to me about shock. I could have stayed in that moment, with no noise, no pain, and no smoke, but I noticed my mum was missing.

"Where the hell is she?" is what I meant to say, though I'm not sure what came out.

Rosie looked up, noticing Mum's absence now too. She looked to me and then back at the flats. Then one of the locals said, "Crazy woman, she heard someone scream and ran into that one," pointing to an open doorway with black smoke pouring out.

I recognized it as the first flat Salma had taken me to, the one with the children's party. Something tugged at me from my memory, but I couldn't pull it loose. I ran over to the doorway and peered inside.

I called out Mum's name, but got no answer.

The sirens were close now. Bull was going to have to move fast to get people away in time. I turned back to the smoke and called for my mum a second time. This time I caught sight of movement. I bent low and peered through the smoke. At the far end of the hallway I could see her, inching toward me beneath the smoke, with a young child held beneath her.

I stepped into the smoke and started crawling toward her.

Then I remembered what was eating away at my memory.

There was a portable gas heater inside the bedroom.

That was when something inside the flat exploded.

THIRTY-EIGHT

It wasn't a huge explosion—the gas canister wasn't big enough for that—but the doorframe shook, and somewhere inside the building I heard a sickening thud as something was forced into a wall. A new onslaught of black smoke filled the hallway, enveloping us. I doubled over in a coughing fit, gasping for air but finding only fiery hot smoke to inhale.

I heard a warping sound and realized too late that it was the ceiling above us caving in. The plaster rained down, followed by wooden beams, concrete, and everything else that had been on the floor above.

My vision was starting to dance at the edges, and again I coughed up something black. As the smoke shifted, I saw my mum again. She was curled into a ball, sheltering the child. I crawled over to them. Mum had taken the brunt of the ceiling, and there was blood on the back of her head.

Her face was pale and drawn, and her eyelids were fluttering; a wheezing sound came from her mouth. She'd been in the smoke for too long. I turned back to look for the way out, but the visibility was zero. The floor beneath us feet sagged, and my brain worked just fast enough to remind me that we were on the upper floor of a poorly constructed building.

It was my fault. I knew the rules.

Get out.

Don't go back in.

Then the smoke parted and men dressed like aliens stepped into the hallway. They wore helmets that made them look like Darth Vader. They were shouting words I couldn't understand. I resisted as they tried to lift Mum away from me. My chest was getting tight, and the world was getting faint. We moved back along the hallway, which was now clear. My feet weren't touching the floor, but my arms were being held up.

Am I flying?

We flew out of the flat and down the stairs. The cold air hit me and almost kick-started my brain. I could feel everything speeding up around me and starting to make sense again. At the foot of the stairs I sank to my knees and realized that some of the aliens in gas masks were holding onto me and shouting. I tried to make sense of what I could see. People in uniform. A white van with flashing lights on top. It seemed impossible to understand.

Wait.

Wait.

Then, all at once, the world I understood snapped back into focus. I saw the cops rounding up people. Only a couple of Bull's transit vans were left, and I guessed they'd gotten most of the people away. Then I saw Bull being bundled into the back of a police car.

Rosie shouted something from somewhere far off. Paramedics had Mum in the back of an ambulance. One of them was bent over her, pumping his hands down on her chest, shouting something at her. Someone else in the ambulance shouted, "Clear!"

And then the world went away again as I blacked out.

THIRTY-NINE

I woke up in the hospital with a scary plastic mask strapped over my face. It seemed to be forcing oxygen into me whether I liked it or not. *Baby steps*, I thought, *baby steps*. I opened my eyes for a few seconds, looked around, and then closed them again. After a rest, I tried again.

I was in a private room.

I'd spent enough time lying on my back in hospital beds. The last time I'd been here, the fuckers had stolen a piece of my intestines. I wasn't going to trust them a second time. I ripped off the mask and climbed up off the bed. Then I passed out again.

The second time I woke up was a minute or so later. A doctor was watching me with an amused expression. He asked me if I wanted to stand up again, and I told him that lying down felt pretty good. He looked old and experienced. The sort of doctor you could trust, the sort who looked like a history teacher.

He told me I was okay. "Smoke inhalation, but could be worse. That'll sort itself out in a few days. I've checked your chart, and you have quite a—eh—*history*. But nothing that'll cause any problems."

"The passing out?"

"Heat and exhaustion will do that to you. From what I've been told, you ran into two burning buildings."

"Actually, I think I ran into the same building twice."

"Okay. What I reckon, and this isn't an exact medical opinion, is your body wants you to stop doing that."

"Yeah, it felt like I was having a heart attack back there. I thought I was going to die."

He listed the symptoms of a heart attack, and I was forced to concede that, no, what had happened to me sounded like none of those things. He said I should stay and get some rest, but that I'd be free to go home as soon as the police gave the okay.

Police?

I decided to ignore his first bit of advice and go for the second. I lifted my clothes out of the cupboard beside the bed and dressed very slowly. My clothes had been washed, or they would have smelled of smoke. I wondered if they did that for all patients or if it was another perk of being sorta married to a top-brass copper.

My belongings were stored in a small plastic bag. My keys, my wallet, my phone. There was what was left of my notebook, and I opened it. At the back was a pouch where I kept an emergency supply of pills. They were still there, amazingly. Soon the pain went away.

I found Rosie in the next room over. She had been given the same speeches as me, but she seemed happy with the former option and was staying put to "get some rest." Truth was, she was flirting like mad with the nurses and was already the hero of the department. She'd gotten a few minor burns but nothing that couldn't be treated with ointment and dressings; she was milking it. I told her about my chest pains.

"I think I had a panic attack."

"You're saying you're a wuss, huh?" If she was taking the piss like that, she definitely was feeling pretty much fine. "Shame." She smiled.

"No, I mean it. I think I had a panic attack. I've read about them."

"Where did you read it, a women's magazine?"

"You're a big help, you know that?"

"Anytime. I tell you what, if it happens again, call me. I'll talk you through it. I'll sing you nursery rhymes and offer to braid your hair."

A nurse came by with a uniformed police officer and offered to take us to Mum. She hadn't regained consciousness, though the paramedics at the scene had resuscitated her. She had a broken shoulder and a fractured skull, and the doctor mumbled something about repeated concussions. We stood and watched her as she drew in shallow breaths with the aid of a mask. Her hand was clutching a stuffed animal, a gift from the child she'd saved.

I knew what I was meant to be feeling, but I couldn't seem to draw on those emotions.

What I was feeling instead:

Anger.

Shame.

Isolation.

Would I have shielded the child like that? That takes something I've always known I don't have. It takes something I've always been jealous of. Going back in for Sally and Bejna hadn't been any act of heroism. It was guilt. The fire was my fault, just as sure as if I'd thrown the Molotov cocktails myself.

As I stood and watched my mother fight her way back from her injuries, I felt less like her than I ever had before. I'd inherited none of her compassion—or maybe just enough to be dangerously inconsistent. Whatever it was that had urged me *not* to kill Mike was what had unleashed this whole bloody mess.

I snapped out of it and realized Rosie wasn't standing beside me. I went out into the hallway, looking for her, and spotted her talking to two women in business suits; their faces looked stern.

It didn't take long to figure out that they were lawyers. Rosie was talking to them about how to handle the situation, which people in the press to talk to, and how to build this into a campaign. I caught words like *media*, *spin*, and *messages*.

I left them to it.

I struck off on my own with the thought of heading to the canteen. Every step I took was shadowed by a uniformed police officer who wouldn't engage in conversation. As I headed toward the bank of elevators, he coughed discreetly and suggested I return to my room.

"Am I under arrest?"

"Do you have to argue with *everyone* that you meet?"

I turned at the sound of Laura's voice. She was walking toward us along the corridor, in the direction we had just come. She took my hand and then pulled me into a tight embrace and whispered something in my ear about how glad she was that I was okay. She nodded at the uniform, and he took the hint and went to look for someone else to annoy. Laura looked tired, and I wondered how much overtime I'd caused for the police force.

She read my thoughts. "It's been a crazy evening."

"Yeah. I got burned, you know."

"So we noticed. You would not believe the chaos you've caused."

"Try me."

"About half a dozen different race-hate groups have gathered at the flats. It's like Mecca for them right now." She smiled at her own joke. "And of course that means national press and cameras outside all the local police stations. Practically every person in uniform has been drafted in, including riot units in case the violence escalates. They're taking no chances after the last time. Becker's unit has been locked away for three hours, going over data, and the council is in an emergency meeting because this is on them."

"National media, huh?"

"You're a star again."

"Human trafficking is hip, right?"

She nodded. "You have no idea. The press love the sexy side of it, the prostitutes, but now they're having to talk about people who are brought in to undercut the minimum wage. You just forced their hand on that. There's talk of a task force. Tony Turnbull, a couple of other senior guys. We're going to have to run with this."

There was tension in her voice, like this was her defensive position; she'd already had several arguments about it, I could tell.

"You're not going to help her? Get them released?"

"How would I do that? This thing is above me now."

"What's the deal between you and Gaines?"

This was the first time we'd discussed it openly, without hiding behind niceties. She smiled and looked down at her feet for a second. "It's complicated," she said. "How about you?"

"Complicated."

She led me to a private meeting room, one of those places where doctors break bad news to families; I'd only ever seen them on TV. It was a medium-sized room, with padded chairs arranged in a loose circle and a table in the center piled with old magazines. The walls were painted neutral beige and covered with posters advertising help lines and counseling services.

We sat next to each other in an awkward silence. I smiled at her a couple times, thinking of a time when it would have been natural to touch her knee or squeeze her hand. The truth was, that felt like another lifetime.

"It's a shitstorm," she said. "On just about every level. The immigrants. The arsonists. The good news is your guy broke about an hour ago. One of the girls came forward. She goes out with the rapist's brother, from the looks of things."

Rakeela. Good for her.

"How about Salma? Connolly?"

"Well, the old man's not new to this. I've read his file. I'm sure he'll survive just fine. Salma's in the shit. She's already lost her job, and she won't get reputable media work again. Don't know yet if she'll face official charges. That all depends on how big this thing goes."

"Has Noah dropped by?"

"I haven't seen him. Why wasn't he with you at the fire?"

I ignored her question. "I have something I need to talk to him about." Then I added, "Are you okay?"

"Me?" She looked at me for a moment. "Oh, you mean my job? Yeah, chances are I'll probably get another boost out of all this, to be honest. Just need to know how to play it. How about you?"

"I got burned, you know."

She smiled and nudged me. "No, I mean, with the cops. You told them anything?" I shook my head, and she said, "You'll be fine. They're going to lean on you hard because you look like the weak link. Rosie's too scary to them, with all her legal talk and media connections. Bull will take a long time to turn over. But you? Wounded, isolated? You sure you'll be okay?"

"Sure."

"Okay. Just play innocent, and they'll have to let you go."

She touched my knee. She squeezed my hand.

FORTY

The police let Rosie out quickly, just as Laura had said they would. I didn't get off so lucky. Not only did they see me as a dirty gyppo, they also saw me as a traitor because I'd once worn the uniform. To round out their opinion of me, they knew damn well that I worked for Gaines and that I'd lied to them about the stabbing five months before.

Most of the questions were coming from a fresh promotion, Detective Sergeant Murray. He looked young and hungry, and he was clearly trying to impress whoever was going to listen to the recording. Maybe he was playing for a position on the task force.

They had nothing to put on me, and they knew it. So, I'd been in the fire. So had the firemen, and they weren't under arrest. I was released, finally, with lots of harsh words about watching my step.

Yeah, right.

I didn't look for Rosie when I was released, though it wouldn't have been hard to follow the media trail. And I didn't check in on Mum. I headed home. I sat on my empty sofa in my empty flat and got reacquainted with my stash of pills. I had enough that I didn't have to worry about getting more. Yet.

I didn't dare look in a mirror.

I filled the room with sound by switching on the television. I scanned through until I found the BBC news channel. They talked about an earthquake in some place I'd never heard of, and an election in some place I probably should have recognized, and then the announcer starting talking about something familiar: a scandal about a group of illegal immigrants that involved arson and riots. The buzzwords were *people trafficking* and *white slavery*.

The news showed Rosie giving a speech to a crowd of journalists in front of the hospital. She was talking with a fire to her voice that I'd not heard before. Behind her, I could see some of her suited legal friends, and for me, it drained any meaning out of her words. It was show business. Saving the world in front of an audience.

The newsreader gave a tidy transition line and cut to a speech given by Rick Marshall at a PCP rally that had clearly been hastily convened. He talked about the fire and immigration. He claimed that his party would stamp out the businesses that helped smuggle illegals into the country, and that the crime organizations involved would be prosecuted. He also denounced the violence. He confirmed that he believed fringe elements of his party had been involved, and he stated that the Community would stop at nothing to bring these people to justice. He talked with his hands and with a firm voice. He looked every inch the vote-winning leader. He'd played me to perfection.

The news skipped on to the next story. Something to do with a celebrity getting drunk at a nightclub. No mention was made of a man being charged with serial sexual assault. I switched off the TV and threw the remote across the room. We'd been wrong. What was worse was that Mike had been right. Nobody cared. We'd done so much dancing around so that the victims wouldn't have to face the press, but it wasn't a news story.

I stood up and headed into the kitchen to brew a pot of coffee. On the countertop was an unopened bottle of Jim Beam with an envelope leaning against it. The envelope had Channy's initials on it. Inside was the cheapest, blandest get-well card I had ever seen. Inside the card were two tickets to the Ned's Atomic Dustbin gig I'd wanted to go to. I threw the card in the bin; I didn't even want to look at his initials. I stared at the bottle for a long time, and I could feel the taste of it. But I didn't crack it open.

I hid from the bottle by taking a shower. The last couple days dropped away as the hot water hit me, and I managed to forget about everything for just a moment. I was dragged back to reality by a violent coughing fit.

As I was getting dressed, the door buzzer rang. I pressed the intercom, and Gaines announced herself.

At least she wasn't breaking in this time.

While I waited for her to get up the stairs I wrote a text message saying Gaines was at my flat, and I sent it just as she knocked on my door. She was wearing a tight T-shirt under a casual blazer and dark jeans. Even dressed down, she still looked better than me in a suit.

She smiled, and I felt something that I couldn't place, and then I invited her in.

On the way to the living room, I saw that she noticed the unopened whiskey bottle in the kitchen—she let it go without comment. I asked if she wanted a tea or coffee, and she asked for a glass of water.

After handing her the drink, I sat beside her. Up close I could see a little worry in her face, a few creases that I hadn't noticed before. Come to think of it, most times I saw her were in the dimly lit club.

"Sorry to hear about Bull," I said.

She nodded a little. Then she said, "And I'm sorry to hear about your mum. How is she doing?"

"Don't know yet."

"They're coming for me." She smiled at me, but it was a put-ting-on-a-brave-face kind of smile. "Bull knows too much. They'll be coming for the club soon."

"Legs? That's off-limits. The cops like it too much."

"It used to be, yes, but things are changing. The police are going to need results fast now, and they know the easiest way to round up illegals is to bust the club. Their stats will go through the roof."

"Are you worried about Channy?"

She didn't answer, but I saw something in her eyes, a flicker of something I'd not seen before. Vulnerability. "He'll make a move," she said. Then she blinked and it was gone. "But he's tried before, too."

"Is this where you tell me I fucked up?"

"No."

"It's not where you say that I should have let you deal with Mike? Or that a lot of people are being sacked or deported because I couldn't deal with a guilty conscience?"

"No."

I looked up at her, and she smiled. Her niceness was getting scary. "I'm just here to make the same offer as before. Come and work with me, properly. With Bull on the ropes, I need someone I can trust."

Me?

"Oh, come on. You've got an army to call on. Just call up the next guy in line."

"You know how to stay alive in this business? You find three, maybe four people you really trust, and then you stick with them. We go way back. You're practically family."

I flashed to images of that party when I was a child. The little girl who was sent to play with me and Noah. Little more than a toddler, constantly following us.

"Speaking of which." She produced a folded sheet of paper from inside her jacket and placed it on the coffee table in front of us. "Noah. He came to me tonight, asking for help. He told me what he'd done, all of it." I winced, and she caught it. "And he's drinking. He's in a bad way."

"And you helped him?"

I broke into another coughing fit. My lungs burned and rattled, and I pulled out a handkerchief in time to catch the black stuff that came up. Gaines just waited for me to finish before she answered.

"I'm helping both of you. Like I said—family." She nodded at the paper. "That's where you can find him. Whether you want to or not is up to you."

She stood up, and I followed after her, holding down a cough. At the door she touched my arm. "I mean it, Eoin. I need your help. Work for me, *with* me."

I said I'd think about it, and she smiled again. A more open smile, like I was finally seeing Veronica Gaines without her guard up. My chest did something it hadn't done in a long time, and this time I placed what I was feeling.

Oh shit.

I closed the door and leaned against it, feeling a crawling in my guts. I fought back a coughing fit. I heard the confrontation outside. Threats. Loud voices. I heard someone get hit, and Gaines called my name. Then I heard laughter and the squeal of tires as a car sped away.

I stood in the hallway, fighting to figure out what I felt. My phone buzzed in my pocket. I knew who it was, but I didn't pick up, hoping reality would go away if I didn't read the text. A few minutes later the phone buzzed with a reminder that I had an unread message, and I caved. It was from Channy, and it was two words.

"Got her."

FORTY-ONE

The evening air was crisp in the city. The fans were starting to make their way to the Ned's gig from the local pubs and restaurants. Most were already under the influence of alcohol. A few were trying to recapture their youth under the influence of drugs. It was a crowd of middle-aged accountants and civil servants in combat boots and rock T-shirts, out to dance the night away, oblivious to whatever changes their lives had taken in the past twenty years. There's nothing quite so dangerous as getting caught in the mosh pit with men who don't realize that they weigh a lot more than they used to.

I was watching them walk past from a spot near the church, listening to the songs and the jokes. More than anything, I wanted to go with them. I wanted to feel at home in that crowd and let the evening take me away. I had the tickets in my pocket. I wanted them to weigh me down. I wanted them to burn a hole in my clothes, anything to show what cost they'd come at.

They just felt like tickets.

In my other pocket was the piece of paper Gaines had given me. I'd read it a couple of times, so I knew exactly where Noah was. But what good would it do? I took a few steps toward the venue and tried filling my head with the lyrics, recalling my favorite songs and the way they screeched from the band's dual attack of bass guitars. Hearing this live music would make me a teenager again for a couple hours. I'd be able to forget all the mistakes and the lies, all the violence and stupidity.

I wanted to go to the gig.

I wanted to go to the gig.

I turned and walked in the other direction.

The city center is an island, cut off from the surrounding buildings and homes by the ring road; it's three lanes of traffic in either direction, and they form a moat of concrete. Some nights that feels like enough to shut out the whole world.

I wished that was how it felt tonight. But it wasn't. So I crossed back to the rest of the world, heading to the train station on the other side of the ring road, crossing away from the city center by a bridge. On the way, several groups of middle-aged men in baggy jeans and rock T-shirts walked past me in the opposite direction. Their footsteps sounded cruel, as if taunting me to turn around and go with them.

At the station, I checked the details Gaines had given me. Noah was going to be on the 8:00 p.m. train to Glasgow. I checked the departure board, and it told me the train was leaving from Platform 2. I walked through the lobby and out onto the first platform without a ticket check. The station had never been big on security. I stayed in the shadow cast by a pillar and looked across to Platform 2.

Noah was slumped in a seat. He was wearing new clothes and had a brand-new suitcase beside him. I thought back to what Gaines had said.

I'm helping both of you. Like I said—family.

Ouch.

He was drunk. Even from this distance, that was clear. He had the poise of someone trying very hard to look sober, someone

213

trying to see the world around him through steady eyes. I turned toward the stairs that would take me over to his platform, but something held me back. Just as I couldn't force myself to go to the gig, I couldn't work up the desire to talk to my brother.

I leaned back against the pillar and thought through how our conversation would go. We'd both avoid the fact that he was off the wagon. We'd both probably avoid talking about Mum. It's the way of things with us.

"How much did Kyng pay you?" I'd ask.

He might deny it. "What do you mean?" Or he might just shrug.

"Did he offer to wipe the debt? Is that it?"

Again a shrug. By this time, the booze would be annoying me. I might lose my temper.

"He offers to wipe the debt and you betray everything you believe in? Your family?"

He'd get angry in return. "When I saw you there, I ran away. I didn't know you were going to be there. I swear, I didn't know—"

"That you would be putting your mum in hospital again? She's still there, you know. She hasn't woken up."

Maybe he'd cry. I didn't think I could take that.

"I didn't know. It was just a threat, you know? Get people out of the building, move them along."

"Just like what always happened to us?"

If I were lucky, he wouldn't ask how often I'd visited my mother before he'd put her in hospital. I didn't want to lose any of my moral high ground. Maybe he'd turn away from me. Maybe I'd say I never wanted to see him again. Or I'd threaten to turn him in.

The Noah in my head came back with one final jab, and it was a shot straight to my gut. "It's what we do, though, isn't it? We let people down."

Ouch.

Connolly's voice crept in, telling me to make peace with who I am. I felt a sense of calm at the thought. There it was. I'd caught a sense of purpose. I knew where I wanted to be. Where I needed to be.

As I turned to leave I saw the lights of a train approaching, and the loudspeaker announced the Glasgow train was now arriving at the platform. Noah stood up with his suitcase and wobbled toward the edge of the platform. I saw him looking down at the rails, and for a second, I thought he was going to fall forward. He looked up and locked eyes with me and stood straighter. We stared at each other until the train pulled in and blocked him from view.

When the train pulled away, he was gone.

Flames rise around the corners.

Dancing red and yellow. They roar like a lion. It hurts my ears.

I'm four years old. This is the first time I've seen my family burned out of our home.

I cling onto my mother's arm with both hands. I'm scared, but I can't take my eyes away from the flames.

From inside the caravan comes blackness. A living cloud that follows the flames out and chokes the air around it.

It spreads toward us. I bury my face in my mother's side, but my father pulls me to stand with my brother. He points us toward the flames.

"Remember this," he says. "Na bister."

Other families gather round. Some of their homes are also burning. Those who haven't been burned out are packing up. Getting ready to move on. Again.

My mother wraps me in a blanket and sings to me. The other women who travel with us sing traditional songs, songs of our people. My mother's songs are different, and she saves them just for me. In a few years I'll understand why her songs are different from the rest.

But right now I'm only four years old.

My home is burning.

It starts here.

FORTY-TWO

I stood in the car park of the Apna Angel and looked at the darkened pub. It was in full lockdown; there were no lights on and no noise came from inside. There was only one car on the car park, the same black four-wheel-drive I'd seen Letisha driving at the sports hall when she'd picked up Boz.

A pub being closed on any evening was a bad sign. On this evening it shouted out about the things being done inside. But at least it confirmed I was right about where to look.

I rapped on the front door and waited. After a couple of minutes I rapped again. This time I heard the sound of the bolts being slid aside, and a hooded face appeared in the crack as the door opened. When he saw me he pushed the door shut for a second, and I heard a couple chains being taken off. Then he opened up wide enough for me to step in.

Boz.

He was wearing the purple and black colors of one of the Birmingham gangs, and he wouldn't meet my eyes.

"But—what about the job?"

He shrugged. "Wouldn't give me an interview, man. No experience. I guess that's how it works."

"So you're back with Channy?"

"Nah. I'm with a new crew. We're working with Channy, helping out."

"But we had a deal."

Boz looked at me like I didn't understand the world, and he shook his head.

"A deal? Gyp, we don't get to make deals. We don't get to choose. That's the one fucking thing I learned from my brother."

I took heart from the fact that they'd left Boz to watch the door. It meant he wasn't involved with the grunt work. Somewhere deep down, I hoped that meant something important. I nodded over my shoulder at the closed front door and told him to go.

"Uh, I dunno, man. I been told to stay here."

"Trust me, Boz. I say when you go."

He stared at me for a while, trying to judge whether he could trust me or not. He nodded and made for the door.

I opened it and waved him off. Then I bolted it completely and stood in the darkness.

There was no sound coming from the bar or the restaurant. I stepped into the bar and took a look around for any signs of activity, but I already knew I wouldn't find anything. I turned and walked through, into the restaurant. The smell of freshly cooked food hit me, and in the kitchen I could see that work had stopped halfway through the evening's food prep. The pub had been closed in a hurry. I stood at the door to the wine cellar and paused for a moment, thinking that I still had a chance to turn back.

I pulled out my gun and opened the door, walking down the steps before I could talk myself out of it.

The room was as I remembered it, the single bulb throwing an unforgiving light into the soundproofed space. The workbenches that lined the walls were covered with neatly arranged power tools. Standing along opposite walls were Marv and Letisha, both holding cricket bats; Marv had a gun tucked into his jeans. They were staring at me like I'd just taken a shit in their coffee.

Channy and Gaines were in the middle of the room. The single bulb overhead. Gaines was on her knees with her back to me. She was breathing heavily and looked to be favoring her right side. Channy was standing over her. A cricket bat of his own was held high in the air, at the apex of a swing, with his shoulder tensed and ready. The bat faltered and stopped as he stared up at me.

"What you want?" Letisha barked. That girl was all charm.

"Sorry," I said. "I was looking for the bathroom."

Channy smiled. It had a nervous edge to it. Gaines turned to look at me, but I couldn't read her expression. Her right eye was already showing the beginnings of a bruise.

Marv nodded at the gun in my hand and then cocked his head to one side. He didn't raise his own gun, but he did move his hand a little, enough to make the message clear.

I smiled at him.

He didn't smile back.

Channy dismissed me with a nod of his head. "Leave," he said. He turned his attention back to Gaines while Marv and Letisha kept their eyes on me.

Gaines tried to call out, but before the full sound formed Marv stepped forward and kicked her in the gut. She fell onto the side she'd been favoring and coughed into the floor. I raised my gun and pulled the trigger.

My arm recoiled from the kick, and my wrist burned. Marv fell back against the workbench and then forward onto the floor; my bullet had turned his left shoulder into red pulp.

Channy turned toward me, but I was watching Marv. His face was white, and his eyes were glazed. He was heading into shock fast. I hadn't heard the sound of the gunshot, but for a couple of seconds I didn't hear much of anything.

In a blur of movement Gaines had Marv's gun. She pointed it at his face and pulled the trigger, and what was left of Marv quivered and then went still in a broken heap.

Gaines had the gun pressed to Channy's right knee when she pulled the trigger again. He screamed and fell, landing on the broken knee with a sound that went straight through me. Neither shot had sounded like Boz's gun. The noises were sharper, like rusty bolts sliding home on a gate.

Gaines climbed to her feet in a manner that would have been graceful if it wasn't terrifying. She turned the gun to point at Letisha's chest and held it there for a second before speaking.

"Do you work for him, or for me?"

Letisha didn't need any thinking time. "You."

"Good. Go and spread the word. Make sure everyone knows there's been a change in management."

Letisha nodded and ran past me and up the stairs, pausing for a second to look back at Marv. All the color had drained from her face.

Gaines walked over to me, and for a second I thought she was going to end it right there. Instead, she touched my arm and said, "Thanks."

I looked down at the gun in my hand. I hadn't noticed until then just how badly my hands were shaking. The world seemed like a distant dream. She eased the gun from me and slipped it into her waistband. Her hand lingered over mine for a second, and she peered into my eyes.

"You still there?"

I nodded after a pause. I wasn't sure how to answer. Then she turned to where Channy was whimpering on the floor. She knelt down in front of him and waited until he looked up at her.

"All that shit you said"—her voice was cold—"about me not earning my place? Well, how's this?"

She pressed her gun against his other knee and then paused and looked up at me.

"You don't need to stay for this."

I thought of Noah, and of Mike Banaciski. I thought of Boz, and Kyng, and all the anger I was carrying around.

I shrugged, and I stayed to watch everything.

FORTY-THREE

I was back where all of this had begun. Sitting in the Legs night-club with Gaines. After convincing Channy Mann to give up his business details, she'd made a couple of phone calls. We'd waited there until her "family" doctor had come to see to her wounds and clean up the mess. Then she'd walked with me to the club.

Inside, the place looked desolate. If there's any place sadder than a brightly lit, dismantled strip club, I haven't seen it. Most of the furnishings had been carted away, and almost all the stock had been removed from behind the bar. It looked a far cry from the dark and seductive nightclub it had been on my last visit there. Gaines explained that the building was going to be having an accident later that night, removing any chance of the police raiding it as part of the immigration investigation.

She told me to take a seat, and I dropped onto a stool at the bar. She fetched a bottle of vodka and a bottle of Maker's Mark from the few bottles that were left and set them on the bar with two glasses. She poured large measures for each of us, and for a long time we sat in silence. I stared at the liquid and thought of reasons not to drink. Then I ignored them all and put the glass to my lips. That first whiskey in five months burned its way down to the pit of my stomach, and it felt good. She poured me a second, and I drained it in one gulp.

My eyes watered a little, and I was taken by familiar warmth. It was followed by an eerie falling sensation, like my soul was no longer anchored to my skin, it was hovering a few inches above me.

After an age, Gaines looked down into her glass and spoke to me. "Thanks," she said again. Almost quiet enough to miss it. I knew I hadn't earned it.

We were silent again for a minute or two. I noticed my hands were still shaking, but not as bad as they had been.

"First time you shot someone?" She'd noticed my hands too.

"Yes." I nodded for a while before finishing the thought. "First time I've ever fired a gun, to be honest. You?"

"Fired one? No. My daddy taught me when I was younger."

"First time you've killed someone?"

She didn't answer. Then she changed the subject. "So, you're coming to work for me, then?" She smiled that dark smile of hers. I'd never been able to read it before, but now I saw it for what it was: certainty. "I'll need someone I can trust."

"After I set you up?"

"No. After you came back for me."

"There's going to be a war, you know. One of the Birmingham gangs were striking a deal with Channy. They'll come for your turf now."

She shrugged, and the confidence seemed real enough. "Let them come."

"You sound like you want it."

"Everything's changing. One or another of those gangs was going to come for me either way. Maybe more than one. Now it'll just be sooner."

Gaines sat in silence for a while and poured fresh drinks. As she passed me mine, she looked at me over the glass. "Daddy didn't get it. He never understood drugs. He thought it was like everything else, like selling more sex or booze, just another business he could take on. He didn't know that drugs would change the game."

"And you?"

"I'm doing my best. The business suits, the whole thing, it's all just playacting, trying to live up to my dad. I had a whole other life laid out. A lawyer, you know that? Got my degree, did postgrad work. Everywhere I went, though, people only noticed my surname."

"Daddy's little lawyer?"

She snorted but didn't take offense. She just shrugged and nodded—that was how everyone saw it. "But when he needed someone to step up, get more involved in the business, it had to be me."

I asked why her little sister, Claire, couldn't have taken over. She gave me a look that said I was the stupidest person alive.

"Claire? Jesus. Well, I'll have to bring her into it now, all hands to the pump and all. But she's a nightmare. She's not got the head for it; it drives Daddy wild."

She pulled a photograph from her jacket pocket and placed it on the bar in front of us. It was frayed and torn; it had the look of a postcard that had been folded and carried in a lifetime's worth of pockets.

"What's this?"

"Daddy's got this thing; he carries an old coin. He says it's the first penny he ever stole. Likes to show it off when he's giving a speech about history and hard work. It's a symbol, you know? Something that ties him to who he is and where he comes from. His father did it too, he says, had a coin that he brought across with him from Ireland. Family tradition."

I thought of my own father, his hands on my shoulder, telling me to never forget. *Na bister.*

Gaines toyed with the photograph, and I got a good look at it for a second. Ransford Gaines as I remembered him from two decades before, with a young girl on his knee and a woman at his side. They weren't looking at the camera; they were wrapped up in one another, lost in a moment. A family.

I pointed at the woman. "Your mother?"

"Yes. She died ten years ago. Cancer. Never smoked a day in her life. I guess guilt will eat at you one way or another." Her eyes watered with tears as she looked at me, then back at the picture. "She made me promise never to go into the business. Said she wanted different for her girls, a different life. But then my dad, when he got sick, he made me promise to take over. You tell your parents things just to keep them happy, but somewhere along the line..." Gaines placed it facedown on the bar and looked at me. "So the coin is my dad's and *this* is mine. What's yours?"

I stared into the mirror behind the bar for a long time before turning to look at her. "Anger."

A lifetime spent running away from who I am. From who I've always been. At least my brother understands himself. For all his faults, he admits what and who he is. I felt like my whole life had been leading me away from, and then back to, this exact moment. Sat beside a Gaines, talking about family and fights that nobody could win.

Gaines picked the photo up off the bar and turned it over in her hand. I caught a handwritten note on the back but couldn't read it. I heard a metallic click, and Gaines lifted her other hand to show a Zippo with the top flicked open.

"I don't know about you," she said, "but I'm sick of carrying it."

She sparked the Zippo into life and let the flame eat at the corner of the photograph. The flame took a long time to take hold, but eventually it did and the young family began to fade to black as the photograph rumpled beneath the heat. She dropped it into an ashtray and watched it burn. She turned to smile at me, and the flicker of darkness was back in her eyes.

"Why did you come back for me?"

I lied and said, "I don't know."

She laughed. "You're a bad liar. But that's okay. It means I can trust you." Her smile again. "Come and work with me."

I put my hand on her thigh, and she didn't flinch. I looked at the smoking remnants of the photograph and thought of doing something stupid.

What I like about you is you're rock bottom.

—Joan Graham

ACKNOWLEDGMENTS

Writing a book is easy. Writing the acknowledgments is hard. Thanks go to friends and family in both the Midlands and Glasgow, for their support, their patience, and the many hours of drunken debates that filter through into my writing.

Key moments of indecision have been solved with wise words from Steve Weddle, Ray Banks, and John McFetridge, with Stacia Decker there at every turn to keep me on the right track. Thanks always go to my wife, but in this case she made one of the more important criticisms of an early draft, and thanks also to Kate Chynoweth for making the right suggestion at the right time to get the book across the line.

The book is a total work of fiction, but there are small Easter eggs in there for friends past and present—if you spot a reference, then it's there for you. Thanks to Robin for volunteering.

I owe this lovely little package that you hold in your hands to the hard work of Andy B., Jacque, Patrick, Kate, Reema, and everyone else at Thomas & Mercer. They do me proud.

Thanks to the George Orwell estate for letting me borrow his words.

Thank you to Rory Connell.

Finally—and always—thanks to Bobby, Paul, Tommy, Chris, and Slim. I can reach for them every time I feel stuck.

ABOUT THE AUTHOR

Jay Stringer was born in Walsall, in the West Midlands of England. He would like everyone to know he's not dead yet. He is dyslexic, and so he approaches the written word like a grudge match. His work is a mixture of urban crime, mystery, and social fiction, for which he coined the term "social pulp." In another life he may have been a journalist, but he enjoys fiction too much to go back. He is the author of *Old Gold*, the first novel in the Eoin Miller crime series, and *Faithless Street*. He lives in Scotland.